Spycraft and The Lash

Scott Sowers

Spycraft and the Lash, a novel by Scott Sowers

First Edition December 2018

Library of Congress Control Number: 2018902750

ISBN: 978-0-9905251-9-6

A production of Big Gorilla Press 2018

"Mystery fans are sure to enjoy the offbeat adventures that befall Rex and keep the suspense going at a brisk pace. And for those of you who like your potboilers on the unconventional side, there will be a few surprises along the way too." – John Vartoukian, author

"One of his sex club playmates is found dead and Rex becomes the prime suspect. As his life spirals out of control his only recourse becomes finding the real killer. Be advised that in "Spycraft and the Lash – as in the nation's capital – all is not as it seems...kinky fun..." Karen Lyon, "The Literary Hill"

ACKNOWLEDGMENTS

The Novels in Progress group remains the most potent motivator for my fiction writing. We gather once a month to review our manuscripts, critique, commiserate, and kvetch. The group has produced tears of triumph and tragedy - both reliable indicators of art production. Without it I would be much less inspired and for that I am grateful to the fine writers who have passed through our doors. Everybody works better with a deadline.

Special thanks to my editor, Jan Arzooman.

CHAPTER 1

Rex's chest slammed into the back of the white, late-model Chevrolet Impala as the security guard pulled his arms behind his back, causing the throbbing pain in his chest to mix deliciously with a shooting arrow of discomfort in his shoulders.

"Ow! Dammit! I told you guys, I'm a fed. What are you doing?"

"Stand down, sir. Don't make pull the Taser," said the guard, as Rex felt what he assumed to be zip-tie handcuffs biting into his wrists.

"Stand down? I'm not doing anything! It is not illegal to take pictures of government buildings! Are you familiar with federal law? Do you realize... OW!"

Rex didn't get a chance to finish his sentence as he crashed to the ground, feeling the air leaving his body, his diaphragm temporarily paralyzed from the shock of the fall.

He lay on the pavement, trying to control the panic induced by not being able to draw breath. It wasn't the first time he'd had the wind knocked out of him, and he knew he just had to take shallow breaths until his muscles started working again.

His head was damp from the struggle and he could feel the

sweat, or maybe blood, dripping from his eyebrows. If he had kept his mouth shut for once, chances are he wouldn't be lying on the pavement, of 10th Street Southwest, in the heat of August, in Washington, D.C.

He could have done as he'd been told and moved off the property or had a phone number in his pocket that he could call to prove that he had permission to be where he was, doing what he was doing.

He considered the possibility that he might have a cracked rib or a laceration on his scalp. And he thought about the embarrassing items in his briefcase that the gorillas in the security uniforms were now moving toward.

He tried to call out to tell them they were invading his privacy, his mind searched for the right words that would get them to stop but he was still struggling to draw breath and no intelligible sounds were coming out.

"Stand down, sir. Do not push me into using more force!"

Rex felt incapable of pushing anybody, anywhere. He watched the guard pull open the zipper of his ballistic nylon, Swiss Army briefcase and poke inside with some kind of metal rod that he'd pulled off his security belt. Rex turned his head, trying to get a better line of sight and feeling gravel scratching its way into his skull.

The guard was now reaching into his bag, while the other four goons watched. He pulled out the paper bag that Rex really didn't want anybody seeing, least of all these nimrods. He was still unable to talk, let alone protest. And then the lights went out as Rex passed out.

When he came to, a face hovered over him. It belonged to a middle-aged white guy, with a square face and dark eyes, wearing a hat—an off-white, lightweight porkpie with a band of robin egg blue fabric around the brim. This guy didn't shop at Target. It was an odd thought to have at that moment but Rex considered himself adept at reading the room.

He spent a good part of his life sizing people up before doing an interview for an article or a TV segment, figuring out where they came from and what their point of view was. Clothes might not make a man but they would usually help you determine what tribe the person belonged to. He was still uncomfortable about what would happen next but the anger had subsided, replaced by anxious curiosity.

"Mr. Armstrong?" the face beneath the hat asked while squinting into Rex's open wallet, which he held in his hand. "Says here you are a federal employee. Federal Development Commission. Is that right?"

Rex spit a piece of gravel out of his mouth, gradually becoming aware that he was still laying on his side on the pavement. "I told them that," Rex said. "I told them I was a Fed. I also told them that as a U.S. citizen, I'm allowed to take pictures of federal buildings. There's no law against that." Rex felt his anger returning.

"Yes. Well. Sometimes the guys on the front lines don't care about things like that, do they?" The man made a motion to somebody Rex couldn't see and said, "Let's get him up and take the cuffs off. That is, if you promise to behave yourself, Mr. Armstrong?"

Rex felt himself pushed into a sitting position and then he was standing, his feet appearing beneath him as the plastic cuffs loosened.

"Ow. I wasn't misbehaving. I'm just trying to do my job," Rex said.

"The officers said you were becoming, let's say 'agitated' and um, 'uncooperative.'"

Rex ran his hand through his damp hair, checked it for blood and was relieved there wasn't any. He then took stock of his questioner.

"Look, Mr. …"

"It's Wellborn, Mr. Armstrong. Marcus Wellborn."

Mr. Wellborn's suit matched his hat and Rex had to stifle a reaction as he resumed his inner contemplations about tribes and uniforms. He saw the inner city population breaking down into two main groups and from there, a few distinct subsets. There were African-American, DC natives decked out in streetwear, which could be anything including gold tennis shoes with wings protruding off the sides, and the other half—white urbanites wearing sensible shoes, department store ties, and suits from the Burlington Coat Factory. This guy didn't fit into either class. But Rex had seen this kind of get-up before.

One of the subsets was your hardcore, proud to be wonks, nerds, and geeks working as stiffs, staffers, and hacks—whatever you wanted to call them. These individuals chose to throw fashion caution to the wind and showed up for work wearing seersucker suits, two-tone shoes, bow ties, and boaters.

These cats were too square to be hip and they didn't care who they shocked with their attire. They cut across the color lines, jumped over party affiliations, and spread out over age classes. This guy was one of them, and that was fine. At least his clothes had something to say.

"Well, Mr. Wellborn. I am a federal employee. I did identify myself. I tried to show them my ID and the next thing I know I'm on the ground, trussed up by the skull-cracking committee over here—hey, no offense, fellows."

"You also refused to stop taking pictures, sir. Which we asked you to do—twice," said the group leader.

Rex shot back, "And you know what? That's because it is not against the fucking law to take pictures of buildings! This is America, and if I want to take a picture of a goddamn building, I will take…"

The head of the security contingent, a big, butch-looking, bullet-headed bald, dude was quickly advancing on Rex and pulling a spring activated baton out of his waistband.

"All right, gentlemen, all right. I think I see the issue here," said Wellborn as he stepped in between them. "Relax, officer. Mr. Armstrong, can we step over here a second? Join me in my office, won't you?"

Rex stepped gingerly over the curb and up onto the sidewalk. He realized the slice of asphalt serving as the scene of his recent altercation was actually an elevated bridge over a railroad track. There was a short concrete barrier wall and a rusting guardrail separating the street from the tracks below, and there on the wall was the agency's Canon digital SLR, Rex's briefcase, and the paper bag. Rex gulped.

"Do you recognize these items, Mr. Armstrong? These are yours?"

"The camera actually belongs to the agency."

Mr. Wellborn raised a finger and tilted his head in a look of harmless curiosity. "Couple of questions and we'll let you go back to work, okay?"

"What are you, Federal Protective Service, DC cop, DOE security?"

Wellborn waved his hand in a dismissive gesture. "Something like that. But if you would indulge me, I'd be much obliged."

Rex looked over the dude's shoulder to see the security contingent, standing in a clump, checking messages on their phones, while the head gorilla stood, arms crossed, and watched Wellborn. Whoever he was, they were taking orders from him.

"Fire away," Rex said.

Wellborn reached into the paper bag and pulled out a plastic 750 ml bottle of Jim Beam with a couple of swallows missing. The placard in the liquor store on D Street had dubbed it a "travel flask."

"You're not drunk, are you, Mr. Armstrong?"

"Of course not. Who could get drunk on that much whiskey?"

"Well, we're assuming you were on your first bottle, aren't we?" He let out a loud, genuine laugh.

Rex was surprised by the laugh and he found himself laughing along until he started to cough. "Yes, I bought it at lunch, I have this chest cold I'm trying to lose and sometimes a couple of shots, loosens the congestion, cough-cough."

Again, Wellborn made the dismissive hand wave. "I totally

understand, Mr. Armstrong. I had a grandfather, ex-cop, used to do the same thing. He subscribed it to 'medicinal properties.'" Wellborn slid the bottle back into the bag like he was trying not to break it, even though it was plastic. He then pulled out the two registered letters from the IRS. Rex had opened them, noted that they were politely requesting a payment of $4,372.00, and slipped them back into their envelopes. Rex studied the pavement as Wellborn squinted at the envelopes.

"These are never good news, are they?" Wellborn asked.

"No, they're not. Some unresolved financial issues with the ex."

"Of course. I don't need the details; I just want to make sure you're getting back all the property you began with. Just two letters, then?"

"Yes."

He was reaching back into the bag and Rex was curious how the conversation about the next item was going to play out. From the bottom of the paper bag, Mr. Wellborn gingerly removed a steel ring sized to a 6.0 centimeter circumference, bigger than a finger but smaller than a mini-chocolate donut. The ring was inside a re-sealable plastic bag.

"And this, I'm guessing, is perhaps something for a securing a boat or a large dog. Curious packaging, though. Just one of these, eh, Mr. Armstrong?"

"Only need one, sir."

"Indeed. Well, then. I think we can both be on our way." Wellborn dropped the steel ring back into the bag and stood back.

Rex grabbed the paper bag, slid it back into the briefcase, and picked up the camera, giving it a quick look-over for damage.

"I do appreciate the help, even though these guys obviously don't understand that I wasn't doing anything illegal."

Wellborn bent slightly at the waist and craned his neck to look into Rex's eyes. "I intend to speak to them about that, Mr. Armstrong. In the future, you might want to call ahead and just let us know you're coming and what you would like to photograph. I can put you in touch with the right people if you like."

"No, that's okay. I have some names I could have called. I was just on my way back from running errands and I need a few shots for a film I'm producing. I'll get permission next time. I take no pleasure in getting knocked around."

"Of course not, who would enjoy something like that? I am wondering though if perhaps we could have coffee sometime or a drink if you prefer. I'm curious about your experiences doing what you do around other sensitive buildings. Maybe we can figure out a way to improve our performance with folks like yourself. Would you be open to that?"

"Yeah, sure." Rex began fumbling for a business card that he knew he didn't have. "I don't have a card or anything on me but…"

"Oh, no worries, Mr. Armstrong. I know where to find you."

"Right," Rex said, as he turned on a heel, anxious to leave the scene and be on his way. Wellborn gave him a little wave and a half smile as Rex headed off.

"Probably gay and thinks I am too," Rex said under his breath as he began hobbling back toward the Metro. The train carried him back to Penn Quarter, where the office was located. Rex used his key fob to gain entrance and made his way up the elevator and down the darkened hall. He locked the camera into the file cabinet in his office and did a quick email check. Nobody was looking for him and since it was a Friday, half the people were off, thanks to their flexible work schedules.

Rex had been with the agency for five years, starting off as a writer on a temporary assignment helping them get their annual report back on track. Since then, he began producing videos after teaching himself to use their cameras and editing software. Prior to this, he'd worked in television writing scripts for home and gardening shows.

His background made him underpaid as a government employee and he was generally under-challenged in his current position. The job was supposed to be a tide-me-over till he resumed his real career. Somehow, that part never quite happened.

The television gigs vanished in the white haze of a relationship gone bad with his producer and prospective life partner who were one in the same person. Working together and living together had proven to be too much strain. She had all the contacts in the business and made sure that he was cast as the villain in the eventual break-up. He missed the income level from his old life but cherished his new freedom and considered it a trade-off that had to be made.

The agency was small, apolitical, independent, and flew mostly under the radar. Its primary function was helping other federal agencies with rehabilitating and occasionally changing office buildings. Rex was charged with taking pictures of buildings, shooting video and producing short, informational films. His background in producing content about buildings and a lucky break got him the gig.

Since none of the bosses were around, Rex shut down his computer, turned out the lights and left thirty minutes early. Another short train ride and he was back in his apartment. He cracked open a beer, stripped, and hit the shower to wash off the sweat and dirt. He slipped on a pair of gym shorts, went out to the balcony, and fired up a smoke just as the phone rang.

"Hey, what you are doing?" asked Lucy.

"Smoking. What are you doing?"

"Just hanging. What are you doing later? Want to get a drink? How was your day?" The questions from Lucy never stopped coming.

"Lousy. I got two registered letters from the IRS because the ex sold a bunch of stock and somehow forgot to declare it as income. Then I got my ass kicked by a bunch of security guys outside the Department of Energy building."

"Taking pictures again without permission?"

"Something like that. I think they may have cracked a rib."

"Poor baby. I've heard bourbon is good for that, but only if you drink a whole bottle. I'm supposed to go sailing with my married boyfriend tomorrow and probably breaking up with him so I want to have some fun tonight. What say you?"

"Which married boyfriend?"

"The one with the massive chimichanga."

"Well, that certainly narrows things down."

"Don't change the subject. Come on, I'll buy the first round."

"Have I ever told you that you're a horrible influence on upstanding citizens like me?"

"Oh, really? And you're what? A paragon of society with tickets to every fetish party in town?"

"That's a research project—but if you're a good girl, I'll take you to the next one."

"I thought you had to be a bad girl to go."

"Depends on what kind of experience you're looking for, Luce. What time is the booze train pulling out of the station?"

"I've already started."

"Actually, so have I. Meet you over there in ten?"

"Dealio."

Rex had met Lucy Wright, whom he playfully referred to as "Luce," the first day he moved into the apartment. He began running into her in the elevator, the clubroom, the swimming pool on the roof, and the bar across the street.

They were both slipping through their 40s unmarried, no kids, recently single, and looking for folks in similar situations. Somehow they'd managed to avoid becoming lovers as the timing of various dates, sleepovers, out-of-town guests, and revolving temporary partners kept them out of each other's beds.

Rex assumed that this would end one day and he intended to put her through the paces once there was a clear path to the finish line. He finished his smoke, threw on a clean shirt and headed for the elevator.

Moving to the city from the suburbs held many charms for Rex, but few were sweeter than being able to walk across the street and into a raucous bar filled with TVs, alcohol, and sometimes attractive young ladies.

Lucy had already staked a claim in the middle of the horseshoe-shaped bar and held up a shot glass for him as he walked in. He accepted the tiny glass of brown liquor and said, "Have I told you lately how much I love you?"

They clinked glasses and downed the booze. "Is that the best line you have, big boy? So what the hell happened today? You got your ass kicked and you were indicted by the IRS, all in one day?"

The louder than necessary jukebox pumped the place full of classic rock as he leaned toward her ear and half-shouted, "Not indicted. What's-her-name didn't declare income and apparently, she neglected to tell the IRS about her new address, so I'm getting these letters asking for four grand in back taxes. Come on, let's get some brewskis and go outside."

He made a motion to Joe the bartender, the universal sign for "two beers and start us a tab." He collected the beers and guided Lucy out onto the sidewalk where tables and chairs offered seats away from most of the noise.

"What are you going to do? You're not going to pay it, are you?"

"I can't even if I wanted to right now, due to the fact the federal government is paying me slave wages for my brilliant work. I have to get another job."

"Why don't you just forward the letter to the bee-otch and tell her to pay up? Why is this your problem?"

"That's another option, but it will mean dealing with the bee-otch, which I don't like doing. I end up losing my temper and breaking things."

Lucy took a sip of the beer and scanned the crowd. "Which takes us to getting your ass kicked by security again. You're going to end up in the hospital if you don't get ahold of yourself. Is that what you want? A little ride to the emergency room in an ambulance?"

Rex fired up another smoke and looked into the sky, picking out some constellations that he'd learned as a Boy Scout twenty-five years ago. Somehow he'd gone from a nature-loving boy from a small town in Ohio to a borderline full-grown, rageaholic man.

"No. I don't want to ride in the ambulance." He felt his ribcage, looking for tender spots. "There was one really weird part about today."

"Only one, you say? The rest of this was normal for you? Is that right?"

"Normal as it gets. But there was this guy, dressed like somebody out of film noir, wearing a hat, matching the suit."

"Bow tie?"

"Not a bow tie, but I bet he has some. Anyway, he appeared from out of nowhere. Called off the goon squad, got me to my feet, and asked about doing lunch or something."

"Probably gay and thinks your cute."

"Yeah, that's what I was thinking, but I'm curious about where he came from. I mean, I think I passed out for a few minutes and when I came to he was there."

"Passed out? Gee, Rex, you think you might have a concussion and maybe you should go get it checked out so maybe you don't die in your sleep tonight? Do you have a legitimate death wish or something?

You know this stuff with you and the ex and the IRS, it doesn't mean anything if you're dead." She started looking at his skull for damage by moving his hair around with her fingers.

Rex gently pushed her hand away. "Stop, I'm fine. It was weird, though, they were taking orders from him like he was somebody, but I never saw a badge or an ID or anything."

"FBI dude, maybe."

"He didn't really look the type—kind of eccentric tastes for the bureau."

"Maybe just head of security for the building."

"No. Definitely too eccentric for that. Anyway, I was going to give him a card but of course, I didn't have one. I hate those wonky looking, G-man cards they give you. Anyway, he told me he 'knew where to find me.' What the fuck does that mean? Who even says something like that?"

"Yeah, I don't know, Rex. I can't account for these freaks you hang out with." Rex looked at her profile in the harsh glare of the streetlights, squinting a bit to bring her into focus. She was blonde, medium height who looked like she may have been on the lacrosse team in high school, definitely girly but with an athletic build. She had green eyes, a nice chin, and kind of a pointy nose that he found especially attractive.

She was a few years younger than him, a Northern Virginia girl with a broken home life and family scars to show. Ten years ago, she married a lawyer who developed a taste for nose candy and strippers. She didn't object when he spent four nights a week at the club showering them with one dollar bills, but she did object when he started bringing them home and her clothes started disappearing. Their divorce was still creaking toward the finish line, landing her and Rex in the same boat, pushing middle age and partying like rock stars—if that's what you called this.

He turned various possibilities over in his mind, trying to picture himself and Lucy together doing the boyfriend-girlfriend thing.

Spending the holidays together, meeting the family and all that but something was holding him back. He was staring at the side of her backlit face enjoying the way she smelled when he felt his cell phone vibrate in his pants pocket. He pulled it out and looked at the screen, which revealed a text message:

"Mr. Armstrong—

Would you be so kind as to have lunch with me, next Monday, Armand's, 801 E Street NW, 1:00?

—Mr. Wellborn"

"That is fucking weird," Rex said. He showed the screen to Lucy.

"Who is Mr. Wellborn?" she said, looking into the screen.

"That's the guy I was telling you about. The guy in the hat who called off the goons."

"How does he know you even text?"

"I got a better one, how does he even know my cell phone number?"

"That is weird, I wouldn't go."

The rest of the night unraveled as most of his nights drinking with Lucy did. They both imbibed too much, joking with the bartenders and making smart-alecky remarks about the other patrons. Rex's impairment increased geometrically with each cocktail that he consumed, until his better judgment convinced him that it was time to toddle off toward the comfort of his cave-like bachelor den.

"Hey," he said, lightly grabbing her upper arm and feeling the soft flesh compress under his touch. "I'm thinking about calling it a night. You coming?"

"I swear, you are such a lightweight, but then, on the other hand, you had a big day, didn't you? I'm going to hang out for one more, but I'm not sure you should sleep. I think that's supposed to be dangerous if you have a concussion."

"I'm pretty sure I don't have a concussion, and I've had enough fun for one night."

"Suit yourself—your loss. Call me in the morning so I know you're not dead?"

"Sure," he said as he leaned in and kissed her on the cheek. "Later, gator."

"What are you up to tomorrow?" She called behind him as he headed toward the door.

"Kinky sex party," he answered back, saying it a bit too loud and at the same time not really caring it was too loud. "Want to go?"

She looked at him with an exaggerated lip-biting posture like she was giving deep thought to the possibility.

"Call me, okay?"

He gave her a thumbs up and walked through the doors into the urban darkness.

CHAPTER 2

The next evening, Rex slipped into his black jeans and pulled the black silk shirt out of his closet. He looked into the mirror at the face peering back. He was reasonably good looking with dark eyes and still had most of his brown hair that was now showing streaks of grey. His forehead was high and his cheekbones looked freakishly pronounced in harsh light. People told him all the time that he looked like some actor that had seen but they couldn't remember his name.

He selected a black-faced watch and snapped its heavy-linked stainless steel band into place around his wrist. After putting a fresh shine onto his Doc Martens lace-up boots, he pulled them on and snugged them up around his ankles before adjusting the jean cuffs over the top. He went into the bathroom and lightly doused himself with a musky cologne to blend into his natural scent. He texted Lucy that morning and re-invited her, but wasn't surprised when she begged off, claiming she had other plans. That was okay. It really wasn't her scene.

The scene itself was actually known as "the scene," a collection of deviants, perverts, kinksters, and fetishists that Rex knew as friends and acquaintances. He dallied with this group when he was married, tried to involve his ex-wife but then gave up when she became alternately bored or appalled by the abnormal behavior patterns. Rex had many chances to abandon the scene for alleged domestic bliss but at the same time knew that he could not change who he was or where he felt most comfortable. Lucy was just another scoop of tasty vanilla ice cream who couldn't quite understand why anybody would do the things that he did.

He grabbed his worn leather jacket from the closet, bringing the sleeve to his nose and inhaling the earthy aroma. He selected his black helmet with the skull and crossbones on the back, grabbed his keys, and dropped the steel ring into his pocket. He downed a shot of bourbon for the road, put the flask in his pocket and headed out. The black-on-black Harley was parked in his regular spot, and he got a quick charge of adrenaline as his eyes traveled from the fuel tank to the tailpipe.

"Hello, my little friend. Let's take a ride."

The beast thundered to life beneath him, 1400 cc's of V-Twin gently rocking in his arms as he dropped it into gear and nudged it out into the night. It was still hot outside, but as he picked up speed the wind whipped inside his jacket and cooled him down. He rolled the throttle back, pushing a low growl from the engine as his speed climbed. He decided to take the long way by going through the park, twisting and turning along the dark ribbon of asphalt as it rose and fell around the hills.

The party was in an unincorporated slice of land out in the suburbs, a cobbled-together dungeon with all the kinky accouterments hiding inside a totally non-descript industrial park. Rex leaned into the turns, feeling the wind on his face and contemplating what lay ahead. The guy that ran the place was a non-judgmental, charming and affable Brit who called himself Chester. He welcomed all stripes into his lair, assuming they were willing to part with a one-time club membership fee of $50. The club had no liquor license, so the bar only sold soft drinks and mixers.

There was a large common area that, depending on the event, would be festooned with stripper poles, Saint Andrew's crosses standing as giant Xs ready and awaiting victims to be tied to its arms and legs. There were operating tables copped from medical surplus sales, overhead hooks and hoists for suspension bondage, or makeshift plywood pillories for full-contact single-tail whipping demonstrations. On any given night there would be fire play, edge play or age play. The crowd was racially mixed and usually skewed toward a younger generation than Rex.

He guided the bike into a parking spot, hit the kill switch, turned off the key and locked the forks. There was a check-in table at the front door manned by a freak in a purple Mohawk and a chubby white girl wearing some kind of a toga, who was staring into her cell phone. Rex pulled out his membership card and flashed it to the Mohawk, who used his black-fingernail-polished hands to put an "X" on Rex's hand with a Sharpie. "First class, all the way," Rex said as he breezed into the hallway that carried him back toward the main space.

There were large screen television monitors on two of the walls, running porno with the sound turned down. The theme of the party was supposed to be summer solstice—even though it was the wrong month—so some of the guests had turned up with halos made from leaves, Roman sandals, and faces painted to resemble woodland nymphs and fairies. Rex found his way to the bar, which was being manned by a petite man wearing black leather pants and a matching vest with no shirt underneath.

"Can I get a club soda, hold the fruit?"

"Yes, sir, and where would you like me to hold that fruit?"

Rex laughed while the dude smiled back at him. "Holding it in your hand will work fine for me, buddy."

The bartender pivoted away, came back with a glass of ice and soda water. Rex paid, tipped and took a big swig out of the glass, replacing the volume with bourbon poured out of the flask.

"Oh, my, the strong stuff," said the bartender.

Rex tossed another dollar in his direction and said, "I'll be back."

"I'll be here," said the dude.

Rex walked away, mumbling to himself, "Where have all the straight people gone?" He turned away from the main room and headed down the hall toward Chester's office to pay his respects. He was halfway there when he spied him coming toward him from the other way. Chester was about Rex's age, tall and slightly overweight with curly blonde hair that defied combing and a perennial Chesire Cat grin decorating his face. The soft British accent was still intact.

"Reximus, Maximus! Oh, I am honored, sir. What brings you out to the hinterlands?" Chester asked.

"I heard you were having a wild party full of naked women doing weird things to each other," Rex said.

They shook hands as Chester said, "You know, I haven't seen that activity happening yet, but the night is young. May I offer you a drink, old chum?"

"No thanks, I'm good. Maybe later, if the magic flask runs out. By the way, I think your bartender has a crush on me."

"Who, Eric? He has a crush on everyone. He's just trying to get money out of your pocket. Speaking of which, by the way, are you booked for the Camp Kink event coming up next month? We have an entire compound out in the sticks, cabins for rent, tents for pitching, swimming pools for skinny-dipping and nearby hotels if you prefer not to rough it. I've gotten Astro-Glide to donate a 55-gallon drum of lube. Can you imagine that? I'm thinking of a giant waterslide except well-lubricated with lube. Epic, is it not?"

"Epic it is, and I'll get back to you on all that Camp Kink stuff. Have you seen the Wild Child around?"

"Amy the Wild Child?"

"That would be the one."

"I haven't, but you might check the back room. She has a taste for some of the apparatus back there."

"I know this to be true. I'll catch you later, unless you're going that way?"

"No, no, I need to visit the main event and find someone myself. Tally ho and catch up with you later."

Rex continued down the hall to the other, smaller playroom, which was equipped with a medical table and a human-sized cross-shaped like the letter T. A dude without a shirt, wearing leather pants, was just beginning to tie up a girl dressed in a purple corset and short skirt. One wrist was already secured and the guy was rummaging through a gym bag looking for more rope or some other essential piece of gear. Rex nodded at the two and stole a glance toward the medical table.

Three people wearing surgical masks and doctor's smocks were gathered around a woman on the table. They were holding her ankles and wrists while one of the fake physicians worked on her lower regions with some kind of unseen instrument. She was moaning and occasionally yelping, which Rex took to mean that she was in the best of hands. He knew from the screams that it wasn't Amy, and he was reasonably sure she wasn't hiding behind the masks, either. She preferred the bottom position to the top.

Rex fought the urge to lurk and watch or, worse yet, move in for a closer gander. It was considered bad form to intrude on other people's scene, although some enjoyed being watched. In the absence of an invitation, he turned on a heel and headed back down the hallway, the woman's moans and groans escorting his exit. He sipped his drink and trailed his fingertips along the wall as he moved back toward the wide-open spaces.

He recognized a plump, redheaded latex-clad figure at the bar—his old play partner, Lola. Once a month, Lola hosted a FemDom event where the ladies wore lingerie and the men had to show up naked—a nice concept, but not really Rex's bag.

"Lola! Hello, darling."

She turned to face him, a vision in tightly-wrapped synthetics, placing her hand on her hip. He leaned over, hugging her ample shoulders and planting a kiss on her full red lips.

"Well, well, well. What are you doing here, Rexy?"

"Same as you, just hanging out and having fun."

"What? And you're all alone? Want to find a quiet spot where I can beat some sense into you?"

"Hah, hah, hah—don't think so, Lola. I was looking for Amy; I thought she was supposed to be here. I was going to find her and take her down the hall and practice my backhand." Rex noticed a flogger laying on the bar, next to Lola's drink. It was black and red leather and its thick handle had a wrist strap and studs for sure gripping. The tails were also red and black and the implement looked to be of better-than-average quality.

"New toy, Lola? Very nice."

She reached for it, her fingers curling around the handle as she pulled it off the bar top. She gently swung it back and forth, letting the tails catch air and fan out in the breeze.

"Yeah, I just got it at this place in Baltimore. Two guys run the shop and make this stuff in their back room. The handle wristband leather and it's a little heavy, but it has a good feel to it."

"Oh right. I know that joint. May I?" Rex said.

"Be my guest."

Rex set his drink down on the bar, stood back, and swung the flogger a few times, the toy making a whooshing sound as it flew by his ears.

"I see what you mean by the heaviness, but I kind of like it. It's got nice leverage. But the true test will be using it on a live subject."

"Yes, well, the proof is always in the pudding, isn't it?"

"Why don't you grab a chunk of the bar, bend over and let me see how it works. It's the only way to know how your slaves are going to like it."

"I don't keep slaves, Rex, but I might make an acceptation in your case."

"It's great to dream, Lola. Turn around and show me how your outfit looks from the backside."

She cocked her head and looked at him as Rex waited for a response. Lola was a well-known top in the scene, meaning she was the one who wielded the whip, but he knew she sometimes switched.

"Oh, fuck me," she said. "You're going to ruin my reputation as an evil dominatrix." She slowly turned to face the bar, reached across, gripping the edge and arched her back, shoving her rear up. "Is this what you want to see, Rexy?"

"It's a start." Rex stepped back and looked behind him to make sure nobody was going to get hit on the backswing. A knot of people had already gathered in the corner and they were now watching the unfolding action. Eric the bartender was moving glasses and stacks of napkins out of harm's way as Rex got himself into position, drew back, and laid a whacking crack across Lola's latex-clad cheeks.

"Oh, fuck!"

"Did that hurt?"

"Isn't it supposed to?"

"Ever hear of a warm-up, asshole?"

Rex chuckled to himself and gave her a few more strokes, alternating where the tails were landing to even out the pain. Lola stamped her boot heels as Eric the bartender watched with his hand on his chin, apparently slightly hypnotized by the proceedings. After five good ones, Rex put his head up by Lola's ear and said,

"You know, I think you'd enjoy this more if we got you out of that get-up so I'd have some real flesh to work with."

Lola stood up and turned around, reaching for the handle, "That is not going to happen. Hand it over."

Rex relaxed his grip, handing the implement back to its owner while chuckling under his breath.

"Fair is fair, Rexy. Your turn." She flipped her hair, pushing spare tendrils away from her face while slipping her hand through the wristband and gripping the handle. She seemed genuinely agitated and Rex felt his mind seize about the possibilities.

The knot of people in the corner had expanded and they were now flanking the two of them, creating a wall of bodies decked out in piercings, tattoos, boots, and leather. Some were slouching, waiting to see something while others whispered to friends. Rex considered the uniforms concept again. Here was his tribe, although a younger version, desensitized by endless hours peering into their phones and allegedly living out loud while remaining safe online.

"Sure, why not. Let's put on a little show, shall we?"

He pulled his leather jacket off, draped it over a bar stool, took Lola's place at the bar, tried to look bored and said over his shoulder, "Hit me with your best shot, lady."

The tails of the flogger immediately fell and Rex felt himself flinch involuntarily. "Mmmph," he said, "Got anything else, mistress?"

The flogger came down several more times as each stroke raised the pain levels. Rex didn't mind the sensation but, like Lola, he was clearly out of his role. The concept of two tops beating on each other wasn't completely unheard of at Chester's club, but it usually happened later in the evening after several rounds of drinks had been downed and the herd of bottoms had thinned, which made hunting somewhat problematic.

"Give me five good ones and I'm done," he hollered back to Lola.

"Count them off, sub!"

The final five were the hardest as Rex counted them out loud and absorbed the blows while trying not to show too much suffering. The pain manifested itself as stripes of adrenaline tossed with a bit of taboo radiating from his ass. Fun for awhile but eventually it just became irritating and he was ready to assume his normal role.

Lola appeared next to him, labored breathing in his ear. "Pretty hot, Rexy. Are you sure you don't want to go somewhere and continue where we have more privacy?"

Rex laughed. "The problem is we both like to drive, Lola. No, I think I've had enough for a while. But I do like the toy. See you around the dungeon, baby."

Rex left the bar with a warm ass and walked back toward the main party space. It was starting to fill up, but still sparse, as the kinky crowd favored late-night action. He sipped at his drink and adjusted his jeans from the effects of the beating when he felt a tug on his arm and turned around to see the deliciousness of Amy. She was younger than him by ten years, with a pretty face, dark hair, and eyes. She could have been Italian or Hispanic; some kind of Latin-based background but now fully Americanized. She was dressed in black with a plunging neckline and, as usual, looked to be up to mischief.

"Well, well, well, I was hoping to run into you tonight," Rex said.
"What's cooking, handsome?"

"I just traded some licks with Lola in the bar."

"Really? What does that mean, who was licking what?"

Rex laughed and said, "No, no, not actual licking. She bought a new flogger, so we were taking turns beating each other."

"Well, you guys really know how to party, don't you?"

Rex wrapped his arms around her, letting her feel the weight of his presence. "Mm-hm, but it was just a warm-up. I was hoping you and I might finish what we started last time. You know, a little public humiliation, right out here in front of Satan and everybody?"

She playfully pushed him away. "You say the craziest shit, Rex. What are you smoking? Hey, before you get yourself all worked up, can you come out to the car with me for a sec? I gotta get my other shoes. These are killing me and I hate this parking lot. It's totally creepy."

Rex looked down and saw her feet jammed into four-inch stilettos.

"Um, sure, but do you really want to change? Those are pretty bitchin pumps."

She was already walking away from him saying, "Yeah? You try walking in them."

Rex followed her toward the door, waving at some other party people he knew along the way. They passed through the checkpoint and were met by the warm, moist air of the night. Rex followed behind her watching her walk as she made her way toward a red Maxim. All of a sudden everything went dark.   The lights went out as he felt himself dropping into a bottomless hole. He free-fell for what seemed like an eternity, not fighting it, just enjoying the darkness and the absence of feeling. He gradually became aware that he was on his back in the parking lot and that Chester was now looking down at him with a worried look on his face. His back felt moist and stiff and he wondered how long he'd been lying there.

"Jesus, Rex, are you okay? What the hell happened?" asked Chester.

"I don't know, I was walking Amy to her car and… Shit. Where is she?"

"Nowhere to be found at the moment, I'm afraid. Christ, man, did you get jumped? Can you sit up? Do you want a glass of water or a drink or something?"

Rex hauled himself to a sitting position. "Did I hit my head?" He felt for blood but found nothing except a slightly sweaty scalp.

"Wow. This is a new one," Rex said.

"Look. Let's get you back inside and down to my office for a second to get your bearings. You're kind of freaking the other guests out. Come on. Up you go."

Chester half lifted Rex to his feet as they frog-walked across the parking lot and down the hall into Chester's office. Chester eased him into a chair, fumbled with a bottled water that he pulled off bookshelf behind him, and cracked it open, handing it to Rex. Then he pulled a bottle of Dewar's from a well-stocked sideboard full of booze and raised the bottle.

"That or this?" asked Chester.

"I'll take the booze. Got a glass?

"Good man," Chester said, reaching for a red plastic cup. "I don't think I have any ice."

"No worries," Rex said. "Neat is fine."

Rex sipped the drink as Chester poured himself a generous portion and took a big swallow. "Feeling any better, then? I mean you know where you are and who you're talking to? How many fingers am I holding up?" he asked as he popped Rex the bird.

Rex chuckled and said, "Yeah, it looks like you think I'm number one. I think I'm fine. How did you know I was out there? What the hell happened?"

"Amy came in and found me and told me you were out in the parking lot. When I got out there you were laying on your back. Do you remember anything? Do you still have your wallet?"

Rex reached for and found his wallet and keys in his pockets. "Yeah, I mean nothing seems to be missing. What happened to Amy?"

"Well, that's the other thing. She was guiding us out to where we found you and then she slipped off into the shadows, so the only thing currently missing is her."

Rex rubbed his shoulder and said, "I am having the strangest week ever, but I don't think I was jumped. Maybe I just blacked out."

"Excellent, Rex. Just a couple of housekeeping duties then, if you don't mind. You signed the waiver when you joined the club, eh?"

"Yeah, um. Waiver? You guys have a waiver?"

"Yes, of course, we have to. The lawyers insist on it. Everybody signs one. You did sign one, didn't you Rex?"

"As far as I know. I'm a little confused at the moment, Chester. I assume I signed your fucking waiver." Rex felt his anger rising through the muddy mind-set he was trying to crawl out of. "What are you worried about? This doesn't have anything to do with you. I haven't touched anybody in here and nobody's touched me—except for Lola, and that was just a casual beating."

"Yes, well, a delayed pain endorphin reaction, perhaps. The point is, I'm a bit leery about letting you, um, play here tonight based on your current condition. You're not drunk or on anything are you, Rex?"

"Why do people keep asking me that? No. I'm not drunk or anything. I just got here, for Chrissakes."

"Which raises another sticky question. How did you arrive?"

"I rode the bike, of course, just like always."

Chester looked at him, steepling his fingers and saying nothing.

"What? What's the problem, Chester?"

"I'm a bit concerned, mate. That's all."

"A bit concerned about people getting mugged in your parking lot with unsigned waivers."

"Listen, it's not like that. Let me get somebody to drive you home; you can leave the bike in the lot and pick it up tomorrow. You may need to go to hospital or something, Rex. Have you considered that? You may be seriously injured."

Rex's impatience propelled him to his feet. "Tell you what, Chester. Check your files for my waiver. If you don't have one, I'll come back in and sign one—unless of course, I keel over between now and then. I'm going to find my motorcycle in your parking lot and I'm going to ride it home, so nobody has to worry about anybody suing anybody, okay? And nobody will have to worry about frightening the other little kinksters, all right?"

As he cranked open the door, then looked behind him, Chester was staring back. "Please be careful, Rex. That's a bad temper you have there, mate. It's going to get you into trouble one day."

"Thanks, Dad," Rex spit back, slamming the door behind him. Rex stalked to the door, brushing by darkly dressed people moving through the halls. He brought the machine to life and roared off into the warm night.

CHAPTER 3

Rex spent the rest of the weekend holed up, drinking bourbon and watching baseball on TV. Even though he'd played sports as a kid in Ohio, he'd never been knocked unconscious, especially not twice in a two-day period. He tried texting Amy to find out what had happened in the parking lot, but she was offline—which wasn't unusual. The scene and the scenesters appeared and then vanished like Brigadoon.

Monday came too quickly as Rex dressed in a hurry, trying not to be late for the all-staff meeting. An unpredictable train schedule and his own liberal attitudes about time management resulted in him missing the first ten minutes—but nobody really cared. His boss gave him a look, Rex waved back sheepishly, and that was it. Deadlines were rigged onto moveable goal posts, and tenured government employees were here for life. As a temp, Rex was more vulnerable, but he was five years into what was supposed to be a one-year gig, so he wasn't sweating it.

As the meeting droned on, Rex pulled out his phone and re-examined the message from Wellborn. So far, Rex hadn't responded. The last thing he wanted to do was spend an uncomfortable lunch with some strange dude. On the other hand, it was a free meal at a nicer-than-average joint. Maybe Wellborn had forgotten about it already or made other plans. Rex texted back, "Sure," and was a bit shocked by an immediate reply that said:

"Outstanding! Looking forward and see you soon.

-Wellborn"

Rex muttered "gay" under his breath while pretending to pay attention during the rest of the meeting, and returned to his desk when it was over. His boss, Lisa, an overeducated academic blonde who probably would appreciate a sound round of domination, appeared in his doorway.

"Hey, so how did it go on Friday? Did you get that iconic building shot you so desperately wanted?" she asked.

Rex fought back a grin and said, "Actually, I kind of got my ass kicked. The security guys over there have no sense of humor at all."

"Seriously? Are you okay? You know we're working with the DOE on a bunch of projects. We could have called and got official permission."

"I know, but that would have taken days. I was right there, so I figured I would just chance it. I may have a few shots we can use that I got off before the Gestapo showed up."

"Okay, good. Let me know if you want to go back over there, and I'll make a call."

"No worries. Hey, before you leave—you don't happen to know a security guy named Wellborn, do you?

"Doesn't ring a bell. What's his first name and who does he work for?"

"I think he said his name was Marcus, and I'm really not sure who he works for, maybe DOE. He was kind of vague about the whole thing."

"Hmmm, sounds very mysterious. Anyway, I have an executive staff meeting in ten minutes, but I should be out before lunch if you need me to look at anything."

Rex waved her off and went through his routine of offloading images, tinkering with videos, and adjusting text. From some aspects, it was a cushy job with a steady paycheck and not a lot of responsibility. On the other hand, the money level sucked and the work was occasionally mind-numbing. Rex clock-watched until a few minutes before his lunch date and headed out the door.

The restaurant was a slightly fancy Italian joint that catered to the office crowd during the day. At happy hour the place was wall-to-wall lobbyists and whomever they were trying to impress. Rex arrived on time. Before he reached the hostess stand he saw Wellborn at a table, poking at his phone. Rex brushed by the hostess and walked over. "Hello again, Mr. Wellborn."

"Ahh, Mr. Armstrong. How good of you to accept my invitation. Please sit down. Wellborn rose slightly from his chair and gestured toward the seat next to him.

"Don't mind if I do. By the way, what was your first name again?"

"It's Marcus—and do you mind if I call you Rex?"

"I don't mind at all, Marcus, but you look more like a Wellborn."

Wellborn laughed and said, "That's fine, Rex. The only person that calls me Marcus is my mother."

The waiter showed up and took their drink orders. Rex briefly considered ordering a beer but opted for a Coke. He wanted to stay alert, maybe cut back on the booze a bit and not give the impression that he needed to drink at lunch. Wellborn went with a sweet tea.

"So, Wellborn, what's this all about?"

"Right to the point, Rex. I like that. Well, as I said during our last encounter, the security community is interested in how we're doing regarding how we deal with the civilian population."

"Right. That's what you said. And when you say the 'security community,' who are we talking about? You're with who?"

It was a typical Washington conversation, where one's life was quickly defined and put into the appropriate box by what one did for a living and who one did it for. Wellborn was spared answering the question as the waiter appeared again for food orders. Rex quickly decided on a sausage sandwich while Wellborn went with a Caesar salad and a grilled chicken breast.

"To be honest with you, Rex, who I work for isn't that important. There is another reason I invited you here today."

"Here we go. Finally, some truth talking."

"Yes. Well. Without sounding too overdramatic, Rex, your behavior and your background…"

"What about it?" Rex said.

"Let's say you fit a certain profile."

"What kind of profile?"

"The kind of profile that is of interest to the security community."

"Uh-huh"

Rex put his elbows on the table and leaned in toward Wellborn, studying his face. The face was a mask of nothingness. No discomfort, no anticipation, no stress—but maybe, just maybe, a hint of excitement. "What the fuck do you want, Wellborn?"

Wellborn laughed loudly and in the same genuine form that he had exercised before. It had to be the most sincere laugh Rex had ever heard. Wellborn tilted his head back and put his hands on his lapels. For the first time, Rex noticed the fedora on the seat next to Wellborn. The color of the hat matched the suit. Under the fedora was a medium size Fed Ex box.

"Well done, sir. Well done. I'll come to point, Rex. Do you consider yourself a patriotic American?"

"As patriotic as anybody else, I guess—why?"

Now it was Wellborn leaning in. He lowered his voice. "As a federal employee working at the agency, I assume you understand the complicated relationship between the District of Columbia and the federal government."

"Ummm, sure. What part of that are we talking about?"

"In this case, we're talking about the Metrorail system, Rex. We believe someone or a group of someones is skimming funds from Metro, and we need help finding out who that may be. We would like you to get onboard what's known in the system as 'the money train' and follow the money to see if it gets to where it's supposed to be going. If you can help me with this little errand, you'll be helping out your country and we would be eternally grateful."

"Wait. What? What the fuck is a money train? Why would you need me? Metro has plenty of cops."

"Of course they do, but we need somebody to represent the federal interest, don't we, Rex?"

"And what, the Transit Police, FBI, CIA, NSA, and the Secret Service are all booked up?"

"A fair question, Mr. Armstrong. Let's say this little piece of business is in danger of falling through some jurisdictional cracks and we're looking to recruit some new blood—as it were."

The drinks arrived and then the food. Rex noted that the conversation came to temporary stops while the waiter was working the table. With the plates in front of them and the waiter out of earshot, Wellborn held a hand in the air, tossing off the tension and lightening the mood.

"I know it sounds far-fetched, Rex. But this is Washington, after all. Everything is not what it seems, and we have a long history of intrigue and subterfuge."

Rex eyed the sandwich that smelled heavenly while trying to plan his angle of attack, "it's beyond far-fetched, Wellborn. And you still haven't answered the question about the 'money train.'"

"Ah, yes. The aforementioned money train. Perhaps you've seen the large steel carts the Metro employees use to collect the coins and bills from the machines."

"Sure, I've seen them."

"Well, each evening about 10 PM, the machines are emptied for the day and the proceeds are delivered to the accounting office for sorting and counting. The carts are wheeled onto the money train— a special train with no passengers, which makes its way down the Green line with a contingent of armed guards who ensure the money gets to where it's supposed to go."

"The guards work for Metro?"

Wellborn speared a piece of chicken off the top of his salad. Rex bit into the sandwich, now somewhat intrigued by the conversation.

"The guards work for Metro and we've received a tip that some of the funds are being diverted before reaching their final destination."

Rex wiped some tomato sauce off his chin and said, "It wouldn't be the first time."

"Indeed. Over the years there have been several incidents of Metro employees with sticky fingers and since the federal government is a major underwriter of the transit system, the American public has an interest in seeing that the funds are going to where they're supposed to be going."

"So why don't you just take this little train ride yourself, Wellborn? Worried you won't blend in? Or do they already know what you look like?"

Again the hearty laugh. "It's not that so much, Rex. A man of my years and experience generally doesn't undertake these kinds of field operations. Recruitment is my current area of emphasis, which is the real reason for this lunch."

"Actually I thought you were gay and was trying to pick me up. This is even more nuts."

Wellborn laughed again, and his hand went into the air. "Oh, that is brilliant, Rex. Quite brilliant, and further proof that we may have the right man for the job. A suspicious nature that goes right to the most sordid possibilities. Tell me, what are your thoughts about helping us with this little dilemma? Are you open to such an undertaking?"

Rex swallowed a bite of the sandwich, savoring the taste of the meat, peppers, and onions as they slid down.

"Suppose I say yes? Talk me through how it would work."

"It's pretty straightforward, actually. If we can interest you in this little bit of business, you would meet me at the Navy Yard Metro this evening at 10:20 PM. You would be wearing a Metro-issued jumpsuit that I have in that Fed Ex box. You would make contact with an agent we have on the train and board as an employee. You would ride the money train to the end of the line and follow the big metal carts to the counting room. Once you see the carts go through the big doors, you get back on the train and ride it home. No muss, no fuss."

Rex swirled a French fry through a small puddle of ketchup on his plate. He really couldn't believe this was actually happening and for a moment considered he was being pranked, but by whom? His eyes quickly scanned the room for cameras hiding near the ceiling or waiters who were really production assistants. Was there a hidden microphone on the table somewhere? He snapped back to the conversation.

"No muss, no fuss, as long as the carts go into the room. What happens if they don't? I draw my service revolver and blaze away?"

Wellborn laughed again. "No, Rex, there will be no blazing away. If you can just observe if the money is diverted and who is doing the diverting, that would be sufficient."

"You don't need pictures of the bad guys?"

"Oh, well, pictures would be a bonus, Rex, but not necessary. We wouldn't want you putting yourself in danger. We just need to know if there is evidence of possible criminal activity."

Wellborn raised his hand and moved his finger like he was counting invisible objects. "But if you were thinking about pictures, how would you capture the images—cell phone?"

"I was thinking button cam. I have one from an investigative piece I did once. It's much more inconspicuous than holding up a cell phone."

Wellborn clasped his hands together and looked across the table at Rex with a slight smile.

"Yes, of course. I'm so glad we've run into you, Rex. Tell me, is this kind of thing of interest to you? Can we count on your assistance? What are your thoughts?"

Rex put both hands on the table and tried gauging his own reaction to one of the most unusual conversations he'd ever had. He considered himself to be a naturally curious specimen, which came in handy in the media business but something seemed phony about the whole pitch.

"I think you're nuts, Mr. Wellborn. I think this whole thing sounds nuts. It doesn't make any sense. Why me? I mean, this is very interesting to me. I kind of like this whole cloak and dagger, secret identity stuff. But why should I get involved with this? I have enough troubles right now. What if something goes wrong? I don't know you, I don't know this dude on the train. I don't even know if this whole thing is real or something you're making up. I'd say, I'll probably take a pass on this but let me know if something else comes up."

Rex reached for his wallet, a bit anxious to put all this behind him before he changed his mind.

"What do I owe you for lunch?"

"Oh, no, Rex. I invited you; the lunch is on me. And I understand your trepidation. I'm sure it sounds like something out of a movie. Actually, it always does sound that way but that's how the movies get their ideas sometimes. The point is, I understand, Rex. I really do."

Wellborn reached into his jacket pocket and brought out an unmarked ivory envelope.

"Before you go, there is one more carrot. As a show of appreciation for the value of your time, we'd be willing to compensate you to the tune of, shall we say, five hundred dollars? Here's a down payment of half the amount. Please take this with you, even if you don't take the assignment as compensation for your time and as an incentive to not talk about this to anyone. Let it be our little secret, if you don't mind?"

Rex looked at the envelope. It was impossible to see what, if anything, was in it. He briefly considered the possibility that he was being watched by god knows who. Was he at risk for something if he took the envelope? Was this really happening? He slowly reached for the envelope, slid it out of Wellborn's hand, and checked the flap—it was sealed.

Wellborn reached for his hat. He picked up the Fed Ex box and pushed it toward Rex.

"You might as well take this too, Rex. A very handsome jumpsuit, made to your size, and a Metro ID badge. Just in case you change your mind. If you don't show up tonight, please throw it in the trash or feel free to wear it. Might make a good Halloween costume or something." He laughed again and Rex felt himself smiling in spite of his suspicions.

Rex took the Fed Ex box and stood up giving him a little salute as he turned toward the door.

"See you around the neighborhood, Wellborn."

"Hope to see you this evening, Rex."

"Don't count on it," Rex called back.

CHAPTER 4

Rex stood on the balcony smoking a cigarette that tasted like pure methane. He knocked back a shot of warm bourbon that tasted like kerosene. As he piled on the poisons, he gazed through the window at the Fed Ex box and envelope lying unopened on the table. He thought about the IRS problem hanging over his head, the lure of what seemed to be easy money, and the pure lunacy of the lunch.

Darkness was falling. He weighed the prospect of more alcohol against the notion of going on a secret mission for Wellborn and whomever he was working for. He fished his cell phone out of his pocket, his finger hovering over Lucy's name. He'd been told not to tell anybody about the proposition if he elected to let it pass by, which was still his inclination.

"Fuck it," he said to himself. He stubbed out the butt, drained the tumbler and slid the door open. He tore open the envelope and found two one hundred dollar bills and a fifty – nice and crisp, the hundreds with consecutive serial numbers. He yanked on the edge of the Fed Ex box, ripped it open and dumped the contents onto the tabletop.

Just as Wellborn promised, a dark blue jumpsuit with an official-looking Metro ID complete with a black and white passport style photo of himself. The badge was stuck to the jumpsuit with a strip of Velcro on the back.

"What the…how the…where did they get this picture?"

The name on the badge identified him as "Paul Johnson."

"Paul Johnson. Oh, hello, I'm Paul Johnson." Rex practiced talking to an imaginary person before dropping his pants and shirt and sliding on the jumpsuit, which fit like it had been custom-tailored.

"How did they get my size?" he asked himself. "What kind of sizes do jumpsuits even come in? Who are these people?"

Rex turned the box upside down and a business card fluttered out. One side displayed Wellborn's name. Nothing else. No phone number, no email, no website. On the back in crisp handwritten text it read:

"Good evening, Rex.

Paul Johnson is a Metrorail tech assigned to the "Systems Division" who is riding the money train back to the counting room to get his car out of the parking lot and go home. Understood?

Tally Ho!

-W"

"Tally Ho?" The shit was getting stranger by the minute, and every instinct Rex had told him to drop the jumpsuit down the trash chute, put the money in his wallet, and forget about Wellborn and this crazy scheme. But he couldn't. He needed the money, was curious about getting more, and he was intrigued by the mystery of it all.

Rex spent a few hours watching television he really wasn't interested in. His thoughts kept returning to how real the ID card looked and how well the jumpsuit fit. He toyed with the idea of dying it black, attaching some chains and studs and wearing it to the next fetish gathering.

If he was going in for a penny, he might as well go in for a pound. He dug into his closet and found the button cam he used when the production company he worked for was doing an investigative piece about crooked used car salesmen. He checked the battery and did a quick test, determining that the system was still working. He snipped off one of the real buttons on the breast pocket of the jumpsuit and substituted the button cam.

At the appointed hour he switched off the TV and took the back elevator out of the building. He wanted to avoid running into a neighbor and having to explain why he was dressed as a Metro employee. It almost worked without a hitch. But as the doors slid open and he stepped off, he ran right into Lucy dressed in shorts, sneakers and a tank top, her skin still moist with sweat from a run. They practically ran into each other trying to come through the doors of the elevator. She stood back as he stepped off and now they were standing on the loading dock of the building.

She stood silent for a second looking him up and down. "What are you wearing and where the hell are you going? Oh, wait. Don't tell me. There's a jumpsuit fetish group and you're the president," she said.

"Very funny. Listen, I do want to talk to you about this but I have to be somewhere."

"Oh, I'm sure you do, um, Paul Johnson. Is that your real name? How did you get a Metro badge? What are you up to, Rex?"

"I really can't talk about it right now. Look, I'll call you later, okay?"

He had hoped to get away from her as quickly as possible, but his cover was already blown. Shit. He pushed past her and walked away.

"You? You're going to call me? Seriously, Rex? Or I mean, Paul. Okay, see you, Paul. I look forward to our conversation."

Rex headed toward the Metro, already worried about telling Wellborn that he'd been recognized in his own apartment building. He used his Smart Card to go through the Metro turnstiles, feeling the cooler air inside the tunnel wash over him as he rode the escalator down to the platform. He noticed that he was walking faster than normal. He checked his watch, which showed him barely on time.

Rex spotted a dude wearing an off-white fedora perched on a bench facing the southbound train on the far end of the platform. He slowed his pace, casually approached Wellborn, and took a seat on the bench next to him. Wellborn was reading a copy of the *International Herald Tribune* and wearing a suit that matched the hat.

"My, aren't we the international trendsetter," Rex said.

Wellborn snapped the paper down and gave him a quick look.

"I'm glad you changed your mind. And it looks like the boys in the tailor shop haven't lost a step."

Wellborn opened up the paper again and pretended to read.

"In a few minutes, a no-passenger Metro train will be pulling in here, Mr. Johnson. The fifth car should stop right about where we are sitting. The train will stop, guards will step off, the money cart will be rolled on and you will step into the eighth car. Not the sixth nor the seventh. Understand?"

"Yes," Rex said.

"Our guard's name is Jackson. It will say Jackson on his uniform. If we don't see Mr. Jackson on the eighth car, you will not board. Understand?"

"Yes," Rex said. The floor lights started to blink red and then white.

"I shall remain here, as I am waiting for another train. Once the train reaches its final destination, you will follow Mr. Jackson and do whatever he tells you. Understand?"

"There's something I need to tell you," Rex said.

A rush of wind filled the tunnel as the train approached. Rex now noticed that at the other end of the platform, a Metro employee wearing a jumpsuit identical to his was pushing one of the large, steel money carts toward them. The noise from the oncoming train filled the station, making it impossible for Rex to be heard above the roar and squeaking brakes.

Wellborn flipped to the next page in his newspaper as the noise subsided.

"I'm sure whatever it is, it can wait, Mr. Johnson. Remember your cover story, in case anybody asks you any questions. You are Paul Johnson. You work in the Systems Division. You parked your car in the lot at the counting house. Your shift is over and you're going home. Once you've completed your little journey, simply board the next train back into the city. If anybody asks you why you're going back, you forget your car keys in the break room at Metro Center. Understand?"

The train had all of its lights blacked out, and the destination windows read: "Special—No Passengers." It stopped in front of them with a hiss, the doors opened in unison as Wellborn continued to stare at the newspaper. "We don't know each other, Mr. Johnson," he said. "Best of luck."

He snapped the paper again. A tall, African-American guard dressed in a blue uniform and holding what appeared to be a fully automatic version of an AR-15 stepped smartly out of the car and looked directly at Rex. All down the platform, a guard stepped out of each car, weapons held chest high, fingers wrapped around trigger guards, eyes straight ahead.

"Holy shit," Rex said. Wellborn stayed glued to his newspaper. Rex stood up and started to walk towards the back of the train counting the rail cars and finding number eight. He looked for a name badge on the closest guard, which read "Jackson," 40s, African-American with a passing resemblance to Wesley Snipes. Spotting him, Rex took a deep breath, touched his fake Metro ID to make sure he was still wearing it, and, looking as casual as possible, stepped onto the train, giving Jackson a quick look as he boarded.

CHAPTER 5

Rex sat in a seat where he could watch Jackson, but his contact for this mission was acting like he was being watched and offered no clues about how things were going to play out. At the next station, the train stopped and Rex watched him repeat the same robotic set of actions. Jackson stood up as the train reached the platform, then stepped out, weapon held chest high as before, as money carts were loaded onto the train by guys wearing blue jumpsuits. Once the carts were in and secured, Jackson stepped back, the doors closed and off they went.

Rex counted five of the huge steel carts in the aisle between the seats. At each stop, more were added. Rex remembered his button cam, slowly reached inside his jumpsuit and turned on the power switch as he began running some numbers in his head. It was an eight-car train and each car held at least ten of the carts. How much was in each cart? A thousand dollars? Five thousand? There was really no way to tell, which made the piles of cash an easy target. Easy, if you could get by these guys with the assaults rifles or do as Rex had done and snuck along for the ride.

At the next-to-last stop, Jackson altered his routine. He came over to Rex, leaned down and said, "When the train stops, there will be a crew to offload the carts. I follow the carts, you follow me. When we get to the hallway to the counting room, the guards will peel off. You follow the carts down the next hall. The employee locker area is off to the right, the counting room is off to the left. If you see any of the carts not going through the counting room door, you make note of who is pushing those carts, got it?"

Rex nodded and briefly considered that he was being overpaid for taking a train ride to Prince George's county—but so what? He'd been taking it on the chin from the government for long enough. The next stop came up quickly as the train halted in front of the platform. Jackson stood up and assumed the position as the doors hissed open. Rex followed him out and stood next to him as the offload crews heaved against the carts, pulling them out onto the platform and then moving them toward a freight elevator tucked inside a dark alcove at the far end. Rex shadowed Jackson, picking his teeth, occasionally checking his phone, trying to act like this was just another train ride. Jackson was the last guard on the last car, the caboose bringing up the rear and keeping a hawk's eye on what was happening in front of him.

They went into the elevator with one cart and the two guys pushing the cart, who were jabbering about who was going to win the Wizards/Bulls game on Wednesday. The cart pushers completely ignored Rex and Jackson as if they weren't even in the same space. One of the cart guys pushed an unmarked button on the elevator and swiped an ID card against a black box sensor on the elevator control panel. The panel beeped and the elevator began to descend into the earth.

The claims, boasts, and theories about the basketball game went on as the elevator went down for a longer time than Rex thought possible. How deep were they going? The doors finally opened with a "bong" and Rex gazed upon a security checkpoint with gates begin enough for the money carts to fit through. A security officer was matched with each gate. Rex watched the cart guys flip their IDs at another sensor and push their cart through the gate. Jackson did the same maneuver and Rex suddenly froze. His mind went blank as he realized he didn't have a card to get through the gate.

If he tried to get too close to Jackson and come through on his card, the guards would know something wasn't right. He decided to use his Metro Smartcard and reached for his wallet while trying to look like nothing unusual was going on. He flipped the Smartcard against the sensor, walked through the gate and all hell broke loose.

Sirens whooped, red lights flashed, and the cart pushers stopped in their tracks. Jackson wheeled around and pointed the rifle at a spot in between Rex's eyes. "Do not move, sir. Hold your position."

Rex froze and put up his hands, one of them still holding his wallet open to reveal the Smart Card. His heart felt like it going to beat a hole through his chest.

"My ID didn't work, that's all. I'm not moving. Everybody stay cool."

One of the gate guards now approached him and squinted to read the badge on Rex's badge.

"Ummm, is this your first ride on the money train, Mr. Paul Johnson from the Systems Division?"

He was black, middle-aged, wearing a uniform, and carrying a Glock in his black leather holster. Jackson remained in position, but the cart guys started resuming their trip toward the hallway. Jackson spun toward them and barked, "Stop!"

The cart immediately stopped as the crew stopped pushing the carts and turned around to watch the proceedings.

"Everybody freeze," said the gate guard. "Now, I asked you a question, Johnson. Is this your first trip to the rodeo or maybe you have some designs on one of these giant carts full of cash? Is that it?"

The guy was now close enough for Rex to notice he was wearing some kind of aromatic oil, like the Muslim dudes sold in tiny little bottles on the trains. The guy was reeking of it. Rex tilted his head to the side, trying to get upwind of the aroma as he felt a drip of perspiration sliding out of his armpit and heading south down his side. He felt slightly nauseous and could feel beads of sweat popping up on his forehead. The weirdest kink party anywhere would have been more comfortable than this.

"No, I have no designs on the carts or anything else. I'm just trying to get home, man."

Inside his head, Rex was cursing Wellborn for not giving him whatever card he needed to get through the checkpoint. He vowed to ask for more money and was already thinking of ways to spend it. Maybe some new cowboy boots, one of those floggers, something fun. A treat, assuming he survived this encounter.

Jackson changed his position, half-pivoting so he could easily watch the cart and Rex. He seemed to relax a bit as the cart guys stood still, waiting for the situation to resolve. But Jackson was still holding the gun in a ready position.

The gate guard ignored Jackson, came up to Rex and said, "Just trying to get home, huh? Well, if you have done this before I'm sure you are aware that this a top security location and your Smart Card is not going to get you in the door. You'll need to use this." He was close enough for Rex to read his name badge—"John Smith." John Smith? Really?

The guard reached for the ID on Rex's chest, pulling it free from the Velcro that held it in place and scanning it over the sensor, which immediately emitted a pleasant chirp. The red light stopped, the siren was silenced, and a green light appeared above Rex's gate.

"Oh, God. Duh! Sorry, man, it's been a long day," Rex said, as he stuck the ID back to his chest and walked through the gate. Jackson looked pissed but he lowered the rifle and motioned the cart guys to move.

"Forward," said Jackson.

"Yes, sir," said one of the cart pushers. "Forward it is."

Rex fell back into position behind Jackson as they continued down the long hallway. Fluorescent lights hummed over their heads as Rex felt his heartbeat and breathing slowing returning to normal. He saw the fork in the hall as guards were, in fact, peeling off to the right while the carts stayed left. Rex followed his guys, trying to look bored; like it was all part of his regular routine as he body began to feel clammy, covered in a mist of cooling perspiration. He closed the gap between himself and the cart by walking faster, trying to keep the foreground in focus. He saw the employee locker room coming up on the right.

The carts ahead of him were being shoved into what must have been the counting room. The crew he was following was making a beeline for their appointed destination, so Rex assumed he was entering the final stages of a goose chase. There appeared to be no evidence of trickery here. But then one of the cart pushers came to a sudden stop. The one on the front of the cart knelt down to tie his shoe. Rex sensed things were not as they seemed. The move didn't look natural. Why would he stop here? He walked up to the cart to get a closer look.

"You guys all right?" he asked.

The guy standing up said nothing but the guy kneeling down looked back at Rex like he was a bothersome insect.

"Yeah, man. We're all good and shit."

"Right," Rex said. He looked down and saw clearly that the guy's shoe didn't need to be tied. He stood there for a second. He hoped not long enough to look suspicious. He wanted to get a quick look around at the space before taking off. There was another doorway in the far corner with a "No Admittance" sign. There were also a couple of buckets, a mop, and a slop sink in the far corner. Rex moved forward and entered the employee locker room, which was empty. He followed exit signs to another elevator, which took him up to the street level. He emerged outdoors at the Branch Avenue Metro stop.

Per his instructions, he walked back to the platform and used his Smart Card to enter the Metrorail system. In thirty minutes, he was back home, where he stripped off the jumpsuit, poured himself a drink, disconnected the button cam and texted Wellborn.

"You owe me $250."

"Splendid! Lunch tomorrow?"

"Absolutely. Same Bat-time? Same Bat-place?"

"Looking forward, Mr. Armstrong."

47

CHAPTER 6

Rex got up the next day ready to clear up some gaps in his personal life. First, he composed an extremely neutral email to his ex-wife, letting her know that the IRS was requesting additional taxes on income that she somehow forgot to claim. He texted hot-little-number-but-disappeared Amy and asked her if she was actually still alive. He invited Lucy out for happy hour after work, while at the same time debating with himself what, if anything, he would tell her about last night.

He clicked his phone into standby, grabbed his briefcase, and headed toward the Metro. The office was calm. All the little Feds were tucked into their offices, tapping away on keyboards or sliding their mice around on desktops. Rex walked through the hall noting who was at their desks working, whose automatic overhead light fixtures hadn't yet been activated and who was sitting around the table in the conference room. One of the people in the meeting was his boss.

"Perfect. I won't have to answer any of her silly questions for at least an hour," Rex said to himself. He settled into his routine by powering up both the desktop computers, the PC for all the agency correspondence and the Mac where he kept all the creative stuff. Lucy texted him back that she would love to meet him for drinks "and hear all about the Jumpsuit Fetish group that he was now leading." Rex chuckled to himself, but he remained mildly bugged that Amy still hadn't texted him back and breathed a sigh of relief that his ex-wife was maintaining radio silence regarding the IRS mess.

He poured himself into editing a video, gratefully losing track of the hours until it was time to head out and meet Wellborn. He felt his blood pressure rising as he briskly walked toward the restaurant, reminding himself that his new handler hadn't briefed him about getting inside the security perimeter of the Metro cash counting room. He had looked at the footage from the button cam and was pleased with himself that it did provide a pretty clear record of what happened, including useable shots of the cart guys' faces.

Rex yanked the restaurant door open and spotted Wellborn, already seated with his back against the wall in a spot where he could see the door. Rex sat down and said, "So why didn't you tell me that I needed the ID badge to get past the security checkpoint, Wellborn?"

"Straight to the point as per usual, eh, Mr. Armstrong? I've ordered an iced tea but haven't chosen a lunch entrée yet. Have you ever had the veal here?"

"I have not. Listen. That whole thing last night almost blew up. I thought Jackson was going to put a bullet in my head, the guys pushing the cart sure seemed like they were up to something and if it wasn't for some joker named John Smith, I'd probably be in jail right now."

Wellborn just listened, waited till Rex was finished ranting, and then performed one of his usual waggling fingers-in-the-air gestures. "Oh, my. It all sounds very exciting, but it probably wasn't as out-of-control as it felt to you. John Smith actually works for us, as does Mr. Jackson…but you already knew that part."

"Works for us? John Smith does?"

"Come, come, Rex who is actually named, John Smith?"

"Right. Okay, fine. But why didn't you tell me about the whole ID thing? Sirens were going off, Jackson seemed genuinely pissed, the whole operation could have been compromised because I didn't have the right protocol." Rex slapped the table with his fingers, a little harder than he intended to, causing the silverware to jump. People's heads swiveled toward them. "I'm going to need more fucking money for this!"

Wellborn's eyes quickly scanned the room but his face held nothing but a beatific smile. He lowered his eye line to Rex and dropped the volume of his voice, forcing Rex to concentrate in order to hear his soothing monotone.

"Mr. Armstrong. Part of this little ritual that you and I both went through was to determine how you would react in certain situations. I can assure you that you were in no immediate danger. We can talk about money or anything else you would like to discuss, but I would ask you to keep your voice down to a dull roar. And furthermore, had you not left so abruptly from our last meeting or not waited until the last minute to accept the offer, you would have been afforded some more details about what to expect."

Wellborn reached into his inside jacket pocket as Rex took a breath. He saw Wellborn's fedora, matching his suit as before, sitting on the chair next to him.

"Here is the balance of the agreed-upon amount. If you think you'd like to take on another assignment we can talk about changing your rate. But I must warn you, with added expense, we expect added value."

Rex took the white envelope, experiencing the feel of the paper through his fingertips. It was a heavy grade, maybe a 28 or 24-pound bond. Kind of a pricey choice for a government agency. Rex wondered again who he was actually working for but decided to avoid the issue for the moment.

"Yeah, well, speaking of added value, the video came out pretty well. You can clearly see the faces of the cart guys, and you can see where one of them faked tying his shoe. There definitely is something fishy going on there. I can let you have the video for another five hundred."

Wellborn snapped his linen napkin and put it in his lap as the waiter arrived. "I'll certainly take that into consideration." He looked at the waiter and said, "I'll try the veal parmesan. I'm not sure if my associate is ready."

Rex ran his eyes down the menu and ordered an Italian hoagie sandwich. After the waiter was out of earshot, he said, "I mean, you could tell they were up to something. It looked like there was a freight elevator in that room that leads to the counting area. They may be sending bags of money up to the surface. Maybe there's a guy on the other end grabbing the bags."

Wellborn was listening to him with one hand on the table, fingers tapping like he was slightly impatient for the tale to end.

"Quite an imagination, Mr. Armstrong, but I'm afraid to tell you, the whole thing was a bit of a ruse. The 'cart guys,' as you call them, also work for us."

Rex felt the earth spin slightly out of whack. "Wait. What? What do you mean the cart guys work for us? So John Smith, Jackson, the cart guys are all on our side? What the hell was I supposed to be doing there, then?"

Wellborn ran his fingers through the air and said, "Think of it as a test, a test that you passed with flying colors, as they say."

"A test? What were you testing?"

"The accuracy of your profile. Listen. Do you mind if we move on? Something else has come up and we're wondering if we could avail ourselves of your services again in the very near future."

"Well, as long as it's not tonight. I have plans. Which, by the way, is something else I need to tell you. My neighbor, who is very clever and observant, saw me wearing my fake Metro jumpsuit the other night. I'm supposed to have drinks with her this evening. How would you like me to explain this 'ruse' that I was brought into by you, Mr. Wellborn?

Wellborn's facial expression remained blank but his eyes narrowed, just a bit.

"What's your friend's name?"

"Why should I tell you that? Are you going to recruit her, too?"

"What have you already told her about the jumpsuit?"

"Nothing. I was on my way out the door. She saw me. I told her we'd have to talk later. Later is tonight." Rex was enjoying Wellborn asking him questions believing he had attained a level of control in the relationship, even though Wellborn gave no visual hint that he actually was concerned about the revelation.

He calmly sipped his iced tea and looked back at Rex without a trace of emotion. "The best thing to do in these cases is to tell the truth. Tell her that you're working on a security-based project for the federal government, which required you to don the vestments of a Metrorail employee.

"Don the vestments? She's not going to believe that."

"So much the better, Rex. But if you're not comfortable telling the truth, perhaps tell her that you're working on an investigative piece about the Metro for a local news organization. You're a writer of sorts, aren't you? You've done investigative work, haven't you? Does that sound more plausible?"

"Frankly, no. Neither one sounds plausible. But I'll think of something to tell her."

"Splendid. Now let me ask you something else. Do you know a chap named Chester Thompson? British fellow, who may be involved in the DC fetish scene?"

Rex felt the back of his neck instantly heat up like an invisible hair dryer had just turned on. He could feel sweat beads forming on his forehead.

"Chester? What did you say? Fetish, what?"

"Fetish scene. I think that's the term that's used. People who are sexually excited by various things slightly out of the norm from—"

"I know what a fetish is. Why are you asking about this Chester guy? Is he working for you, too?"

Wellborn laughed. "You really are too much, Mr. Armstrong. I couldn't tell you that even if it were true. I'd have to kill you or something." More laughter.

Wellborn was laughing so hard his eyes were watering. Rex weighed his options for divulging more information that he really didn't want to share, just as the food arrived. "Thank god," he said to himself. He focused on his sandwich, hoping Wellborn would change the subject, which did not happen. Wellborn began dissecting his slab of veal with surgical skill as the next question popped out.

"But seriously, Rex, Mr. Thompson finds himself in between and betwixt a number of people of interest to us. If you do, in fact, know him, and I'm not judging how or why you would know such an individual, there are certain things that might be worth a rise in your day rate. If you, in the parlance of the times, catch my drift."

Rex swallowed a bite of sandwich then washed it down with some Coke, wishing it were an amped-up, micro-brewed IPA. He cleared his throat and said, "First of all, Mr. Wellborn, 'catch my drift,' isn't exactly the parlance of the times. Maybe twenty years ago, and I do appreciate the pop culture reference, but nobody says that anymore. Second of all, I call bullshit, on this, 'do you happen to know Chester Thompson?' malarkey. Obviously you know I know him, otherwise, you wouldn't have just pulled this name out of nowhere. So what it is that you really want to know about Chester and the fetish scene? Let's stop fucking around with each other, shall we?" It came out sounding a bit more hostile than Rex wanted and he felt a wave of regret wash over him.

Wellborn stopped slicing his veal, holding the steak knife up an angle where Rex could see Wellborn's face reflected in the blade. His visage seemed the same unreadable mask it had been at each of their meetings. But for a second Rex saw something in his eyes that betrayed a grandmaster of illusion and misdirection. Rex's gaze traveled from the knife back to Wellborn's face. His perception of the overly-formal, fedora-wearing, fuddy-duddy morphed into an image of a cold-blooded killer. His face seemed harder and there was something about the way he held the knife that looked threatening while maintaining totally socially acceptable table manners. Who was this guy?

For a moment Rex considered the possibility that a highly skilled, sociopath assassin sat across the table from him, chuckling, laughing, and throwing out suppositions about this and that. But under the façade, there was a steel column of resolve.

"Tell you what, Rex. Let's table that discussion for a moment, shall we? I need to find out a bit more about what we want to know about what, and I can tell this is a sensitive subject for you. In the meantime, I'm wondering if you could join me at the corner of M and 2nd, Southeast, tomorrow evening, say around seven? Your next task for us, assuming you want to continue on, would involve going inside a building near that location and having a look around. The job would pay double your last rate, but the safety net wouldn't be quite so, shall we say, accommodating. What say you, Mr. Armstrong? Like to take it up a notch?" Wellborn stuck out his chin, waiting for a response.

Rex tried to juxtapose the calm setting of the restaurant, Wellborn's nonplussed nature, and the total normalness of the business-as-usual lunch scene going on around him, with the fact that the guy in the funny hat had somehow crawled deep into his skull very quickly, asking questions about things that he shouldn't actually know anything about.

"What's at the corner of M and 2nd? That's not far from where I live. What is that, a government office building?"

"It's close to several federal buildings." Wellborn gently laid his flatware down on the linen tablecloth and said, "Look, Rex. I hate to be a stickler, but I need to know your interest level before I reveal too many details about the situation. If you decline, I need to hire another operative, and then the trail of information becomes," he wiggled his fingers in the air, "untidy."

Rex bit the head off a French fry. He zeroed in on Wellborn's tie and shirt, both of which were totally forgettable. But the hat, the jacket, and the trousers all working together to form this vision of what? He didn't fully understand the mind-set of this tribe of eccentric dressers. Were they trying to call attention to themselves? Rebelling a bit against more mundane business attire in their own quirky way? A fetish of its own, perhaps?

"And we're talking, what? A thousand dollars? And what do I have to do at the corner of M and 2nd to make a thousand dollars?"

Wellborn pursed his lips and said nothing. Rex felt a pressure building at the table. An uncomfortable silence hung between the two men, the bubble gradually getting bigger and bigger, the skin stretching to contain the discomfort growing between them.

Rex knew he was feeling the pressure but Wellborn looked cool. The moment stretched as Rex continued to say nothing. His mind flashed back to an episode of his past where he tried his hand at selling cars one of his first jobs out of college. He remembered the sales manager advising that when trying to close a deal, he should ask the customer for the sale and then say nothing. Whoever spoke next, lost.

In this situation with Wellborn he'd already decided to see how long he could go with saying anything, trying to gain some kind of edge in the conversation. Wellborn let out an audible breath as if he had assumed the silence was a decline. He picked up his fork and began eating again.

"Okay, fine," Rex said. "I'll do it. I just wish I knew what I'm agreeing to do." He needed the money, the location was right across the street and his curiosity was getting the better of him.

"All in due time. Your patience shall be rewarded."

Rex finished his meal and said goodbye to Wellborn, after double-checking where and when he was supposed to be to start his next mission. He pulled the envelope out of his pocket and verified two hundreds and a fifty He folded the cash into his wallet. His head was swimming a bit as he tried to make some kind of sense from the new information. How did Chester fit in with this? Did the Feds know that he was involved in the scene? Could he lose his job over this? What the hell was he actually going to tell Lucy?

Once back in the office he dove into his work, trying to ignore the non-work activity going on around him. An email showed up in his inbox inviting him to an event sponsored by the "Social Committee." The parade of birthday parties, retirement functions, and baby showers never stopped. The receptionist was always going door to door, passing a hat. Cards needed to be signed and cake had to be eaten. He took a break, rubbing his eyes, and said to himself, "This is why nothing ever gets done in the government; everybody is too busy planning parties instead of actually working."

"Knock-knock." It was his boss, who had somehow appeared in his doorway without making her presence known.

"Oh, hi there," he said. "I didn't hear you come in." She leaned against the doorframe and crossed her ankles.

"Obviously. Were you just talking to yourself about going to parties?"

"Yeah, sorry. I'm still not used to this office environment where people spend so much time celebrating life's little milestones. There's just no end to them."

"We all can't be as cool and hip as you, Rex. Some of these people consider themselves part of an office family and families celebrate."

"With cake."

"Yes. With cake, and sometimes ice cream, if we're lucky. How's the DOJ video coming? Anything for me to look at?"

"It's almost there. Can I show you tomorrow?"

"Sure. And try to get some rest tonight, Rex. You look kind of tired."

"I'll sleep when I'm dead."

"Oh, one more thing. Did you tell me last week you had some

kind of a run-in with a security guy named Wellborn?"

Rex felt himself swallow involuntarily. "Yeah, why?"

"Did you tell him you were working for me? Because he sent me an email asking to see if you were available to serve on a special detail reviewing security protocols around federal buildings, or something like that."

"Really. What did you tell him?"

"I told him it was fine as long as it didn't interfere with your duties here. He was very polite and spoke highly of you in the email."

"That sounds like him. So what agency does he actually work for?"

"That's a good question. He had a .gov email address but there was no signature on the email saying exactly who he works for. Weird, huh?"

Rex swallowed again. "Yeah, it is weird, and he is very polite. Wow."

"Yeah. Anyway, I'll let you know if he emails again or calls, and if he contacts you directly, just let me know what's going on so I can adjust the schedule."

"Right. Okay. Sure, will do."

"Making friends everywhere you go, aren't you, Rex? Roughed up by security and then special-detailed."

"I reckon."

She gave Rex a little smile, turned, and was gone down the hallway without a sound. As the clock struck six, he was out the door and making final arrangements with Lucy via text. He rode the train home, pulled off his work costume and changed into black jeans, engineer boots, and a t-shirt. He purposely did not think about what he was going to tell Lucy, preferring to put himself into the moment of the situation and see what came out. He pulled a bottle of vodka out of the freezer and poured himself a healthy shot, watching the thick, clear liquid coming out of the bottle like 90-proof syrup. He took the shot on the balcony, washed it down with a quick smoke, brushed his hair back, and headed to the bar.

He walked the long way around the block, making his way to the corner of 2nd and M. Standing on the corner and scanning revealed the Department of Transportation, a CVS, a bank, and the abandoned headquarters of the Geospatial Intelligence Agency.

"What the fuck?" Rex said to himself and to any of the office drones passing within earshot. "What the hell could possibly be of any interest here and what does this have to do with missing Metro money?"

He turned on his heel and walked straight to the bar. Inside, knots of dudes with ties slightly askew stood and yelled at each other about what sports team was going to do to another sports team, or made declarations of past drunkenness, or loudly voiced opinions about the moral compasses of various workmates. The barstools were filled with more dudes staring into cell phones as if the secrets of the universe were about to be revealed. Standing in the spot where the waitresses came to pick up their orders was Lucy, raising what appeared to be a shot of bourbon in his direction.

"Hello, my dear," he said as took the shot out of her hand and downed it in one smooth motion. Her empty shooter indicated that she was that much ahead of him.

"Well, well, well, if it isn't Mr. Metro himself. What's happening, Rex?"

Rex held up a finger to signal, "hold that thought," ordered two beers, and pulled her by the elbow to a quieter table outside. He shook a cigarette out of the pack and proceeded to tell her the whole, entire truth about everything that had happened to him over the past 72 hours.

"Wow," she said. "That is quite a story, even for you. So the girl you were trying to get with at the club, no sign of her?"

"Not a peep."

"And this Wellborn guy, still no clue about who he works for?"

"Not a clue."

"But he did pay you?"

"Paid in full."

"And he wants you to do something-something near the corner, right here, right down the street?"

"Right down the street."

"And this Chester guy, the fetish king, you think he's really a Russian spy or something?"

"Actually, he's British."

"And you think Wellborn called your boss to make sure it was okay to send you off on other secret agent missions?"

"Actually, he emailed her without identifying who he actually works for—again."

"Are you taking drugs, Rex, or is there any history of mental illness in your family?"

He laughed.

"I'm serious. This is all a bit beyond belief. Assuming you're not crazy, are you even supposed to be telling anybody about this?"

"I told Wellborn you saw me in the Metro get-up and asked him what I should do. He said the best thing to do in these cases is to tell the truth."

"And that's what you're doing now. You're telling the truth?"

"Quite correct, Luce. I am, in fact, telling the truth."

"First of all, I'm not sure I want you talking to Wellborn about me. Second of all, I'm getting another beer, you want one?"

"Sure." Rex said as he felt his phone vibrate. He watched Lucy pull herself away from the table and looked at his phone, which revealed a text from his ex-wife.

"You and your friends at the IRS can go fuck yourselves."

"Perfect," he said as he tossed the phone onto the tabletop.

CHAPTER 7

Rex woke up feeling fairly clear, considering his level of intake the night before. He had a productive morning at work, showed his boss the latest version of the video he was working on, got some reasonable feedback, and went to lunch. The rest of the day went quickly and he found himself walking toward the appointed meeting place feeling purposeful and relaxed.

There was a Metro stop on the northeast corner of the intersection where he was supposed to meet his guy. As he approached, Rex saw Wellborn sitting on one of the benches reading a copy of the *Wall Street Journal*. Rex took a seat next to him. "Checking your portfolio, Wellborn?"

Wellborn closed the paper. "Something like that. A timely appearance, Mr. Armstrong. I admire your punctuality. That's hard to come by these days."

"Indeed it is, Mr. Wellborn. So what's the caper?"

Wellborn laughed his hearty laugh. "Well done, sir," he said. "Well done. The caper, as you put it, involves what happens on the top floor of the building across the street."

"The CVS?"

"Look up. Up above the drug store."

Rex followed his instructions and for the first time noticed the CVS was on the ground floor of a building with a giant aluminum logo on the top that said, "ETRANGER."

"Okay, so what is it or who is it?" Rex asked.

"Defense contractor. French. The word means 'alien' in French."

"Really? What the hell is a French defense contractor doing with a building here?"

"Oh, they're everywhere, Rex. The Frenchies stay quite busy selling arms to feuding groups everywhere. We collaborate with them on certain things and compete on others. It's all quite incestuous, I'm afraid."

"Seriously? The French?"

"Quite serious, Rex. Anyway, do you see the room on the top floor, near the middle of the building, with what appears to be neon lights attached to the ceiling?"

Rex found the room that Wellborn was talking about. "Huh," he said.

"Yes, well. That room is used for entertaining clients, customers, visiting dignitaries, that kind of thing. There's an affair up there this evening and we would like you to attend on our behalf." Rex reached into his jacket pocket and pulled out an envelope. "The envelope contains one half of our agreed-upon fee, an invitation that will get you into the affair, and some images of people. We would like you to go in and see if any of the people in the pictures show up for the party and who they talk to. You'll need to stay until the party breaks up. They'll be a mix of important people and not-so-important staffers from various government agencies, so you'll blend in. You can tell people who you are and the agency you work for in real life. Chances are nobody will care. Do you speak French, by any chance?"

"Not really," Rex said.

Wellborn waved his finger in the air. "No matter; the generals don't either."

"Generals?"

"Oops. Did I say, generals?" Wellborn made an exaggerated gesture of putting his hand over his mouth as if he had just spilled the beans. He laughed again as he folded his newspaper with great care. "Yes, I'm afraid some of our generals may be selling drone technology to the French. Shocking, eh, Mr. Armstrong?"

"Our generals? And the French? We're spying on our own generals and the French? Is that what you're telling me?"

"Yes. Well, we have a long history of spying on the French, and as for the military, you never can trust those buggers either. So much money involved, isn't there? The party starts at seven. You may want to ditch your briefcase, change into something a bit more party-like, and head over. I shall debrief you tomorrow at lunch. Will that work for you?"

"Um, yeah, sure." Rex tucked the envelope into his jacket pocket. "Do you want me to engage the generals or anything like that?"

"No engagement is necessary. We just want to know if they're in the room. Bonus points if you can overhear what they're talking about and who they are talking to. That is all."

"Done and done," Rex said. He and Wellborn rose from the bench. "Same time, same station for lunch?

"I shall look forward to it. Fare thee well and Godspeed," Wellborn said.

"Cheers," Rex said. He turned and headed back to the apartment. He got to the elevator, pushed the button, the doors opened, and there was Lucy.

"Well, well, well—going up, young man?"

Rex stepped into the elevator. "I am, actually. What are you up to?"

"So far, not a thing. You?"

"I just got another assignment—to go to a party across the street."

"A party, you say? Kinky Metro workers in jumpsuits? That kind of thing?"

"Actually, American generals and French defense contractors. Want to go?"

"Why, thank you, Rex. I would love to. What's the dress code?"

She was smirking and Rex loved it when she acted overly formal, so prim and proper. The desire to corrupt her was hard to ignore even if she was faking a bit.

The elevator reached his floor and the doors slid open.

"Business casual. Meet me in the lobby at ten to seven if you're serious."

"Oh, I'm serious, Rex. Very serious." She gave him a wink as he stepped out. As he headed toward his apartment, he wondered what the hell he was doing. Sometimes the things that came out of his mouth surprised him—like he was watching himself walking around doing and saying things.

As he changed shirts and fluffed his hair his mind veered off in the other direction, thinking it might be better if he took a date to this party or whatever it was. It would look more natural if he had somebody to talk to. Plus, two of them could work the room and Lucy could see that he wasn't making the whole thing up.

He ripped open the envelope and dumped the contents on the table. There were five one hundred dollar bills, which caused the phrase, "I just printed these," to pop into his head. There also was an invitation from the Etranger Corporation for a cocktail party, and three Polaroid pictures of guys in uniforms posing with men in expensive-looking suits.

"Polaroids? What century are these guys operating in?" Rex said to himself. He tucked the bills into his wallet, slipped the pictures into his jacket pocket, and checked his hair in the mirror. He poured himself a drink and powered up the computer to check out Etranger's online presence. The site was mostly in French and seemed to be vague on purpose. He checked the time, finished the drink, and headed downstairs. Lucy was waiting in the lobby in a flouncy white dress. Tasteful—yet sexy, Rex thought.

"Wow," he said.

"Too much?"

"Not for me, baby."

"How are we traveling?"

"It's walkable. Are you sure you want to do this?"

"Gee, I don't know Rex, do you think it's dangerous?"

Rex could tell she wasn't completely convinced he was telling the truth. He smiled to himself and touched her elbow, steering her toward the back door. "I doubt that. They sent me some Polaroids. U.S. generals who are maybe selling drone secrets to the French. A French defense contractor has an office right across the street above the CVS."

They walked toward the back door of the building. "I see," Lucy said. "Well, that all makes perfect sense. And so you and the Mission Impossible team are being sent into the CVS to break up the spy ring—is that it?"

"Something like that, yeah."

Rex went into the CVS at least twice a week. He hated the store as it was always under-stocked and "clogged up with stupid people trying to buy things" – a phrase he filched from his ex, one of the few things he deemed worthy of holding onto. It was the closest place to buy items essential to urban survival. Yet he'd never noticed the main entrance to the building, which was located in the middle of the structure. Rex pulled open a heavy glass door. Looking around, he noticed a security camera dome in the corner of the foyer. He checked the invitation, which directed him to the

13th floor.

The hallway led them toward a security desk. There were two guards in uniforms behind the desk and a dude in a tailored suit standing next to it with his hands clasped in front of him. He wore an earpiece, its cord disappearing inside the suit. Rex looked for the bulge of a pistol near the guy's rib cage, but couldn't see anything suspicious.

Rex pulled out the invitation and looked from the guy in the suit to the uniformed guards and said, "Etranger?" He did his best to put a French accent on the word.

"Of course, sir," said the suit guy, who didn't have to fake an accent. "IDs, please."

Rex and Lucy pulled out their driver's licenses and handed them over. The suit guy wrote their names onto a columned piece of paper and gestured toward the elevators. "Thirteenth floor— enjoy your evening." After the elevator doors closed, Lucy said, "Well, that seemed very official and all. Who knew a nest of French spies was lurking right across the street."

"Actually, we would be the spies in this case. We are spying on them."

"Right. Got it."

The elevator doors opened to a nondescript-looking hallway, but there was cool jazz coming from somewhere nearby. There was a sign on an easel directing them toward a room where Rex could see people milling about. They walked down with Rex gently laying his hand on Lucy's back, feeling the muscles rising and falling as she walked, her heels clicking on the stone floor. He thought about her in a lacrosse uniform, her hair pulled back into a ponytail. She accepted his touch and said, "It's a cocktail party, so there will be cocktails, right?"

"I'm sure."

They walked through the doorway into a nicely paneled boardroom. Buffet tables lined both walls and held steaming chafing dishes. There were plates of cheese and fruit, and a dessert section. A three-piece combo was set up on a small stage in one corner of the room, and there was a bar with uniformed bartenders positioned at each of the far ends.

Rex looked at the ceiling and realized the blue lights he'd seen from the street were actually coming from an adjacent kitchen used for catering the event. There were clumps of people in the semi-darkened space chatting, laughing, checking their phones, and looking around to see who else was there.

"Whoa," Lucy said. "Some spread. Come on, I'll buy you a drink."

They walked toward the bar. Rex scanned the faces for the guys he was looking for. They reached the bar and ordered drinks as Lucy said, "So let me help you. Show me the shots of the guys." Rex pulled out the pictures and handed them over.

"They really are Polaroids. I didn't know they still made those."

"I know, right? Maybe they use them because there are no digital copies. It's some kind of retro, old-school way of keeping track of who has the images." Rex sipped his drink and felt his phone vibrate. He checked the number and didn't recognize it, which usually meant letting it go to voicemail. But for whatever reason, he decided to answer. "Hello?"

A familiar voice with a British accent said, "Is that you, Rex? It's Chester Thompson."

"You found me, Chester. What's up?"

"Just checking in, mate; how are you feeling? Any more health issues since we saw you last?"

"No, no, I'm fine. Listen, Chester. I'm kind of in the middle of something here. Any chance I can call you back?"

"Actually, I'm in the middle of something myself. This won't take long and I'm afraid I have some disturbing news. Are you alone?"

Rex started walking back toward the entrance, waving off Lucy.

"I will be in a second…why? What's going on?" Rex felt his heartbeat quickening involuntarily as his head swam a bit. Now what?

"It's about your little friend from the other night. Amy?"

"Amy. Yes, I've been texting her but she hasn't responded. Have you talked to her? "

"Not exactly, Rex. Listen there's no easy way to say this but I just spent an hour with the DC coppers, who told me she's dead. The last time anybody saw her alive was in here on Saturday night. They think somebody killed her."

Rex slumped against the hallway wall, absorbing the news.

"What did you say? Did you say 'dead'? Are you sure?"

"They showed me pictures, mate. It was her and she had one of my club ID cards on her. Look. Here's the thing. I had to tell them you were here and that you blacked out—or whatever happened to you in the parking lot. I'd be expecting a visit from them sooner rather than later."

"Wait. You told them what?" The phone beeped like it lost the connection and then went dead. Rex slipped the phone back into his pocket. He looked up at the acoustical tile ceiling, feeling his mind go blank for a second. Then the questions started coming. "What the hell is going on?" he asked himself. "Did Chester give them his contact info? Wasn't that protected by scene protocol or something? Did he need a lawyer?"

He walked back into the room in a daze, the phone still warm in his pocket. Lucy was still at the bar, doing a rotten job of looking at the pictures while trying to pretend that she wasn't looking at the pictures.

Rex moved in next to her to help shield her from prying eyes and ordered a fresh drink.

"Who was that, your crazy ex?" asked Lucy.

"No. It was a stranger call than that. A girl I know was killed last week. The one I was telling you about. I mean, I just saw her on Saturday."

Lucy turned to him and said, "What? What do you mean, 'killed'? Killed, like in, dead?"

"Yes. Killed like in dead."

"My god, that's horrible. Did you know her well?"

"Not that well, but still. It's freaky, right? Maybe Chester's confused, or it's a prank or something."

"If it's a prank, it's a totally sick prank to play on anybody."

"Yeah, I agree, totally fucked up." Rex ran his hand across his forehead, took a big sip from his drink and scanned the room, trying to refocus on the job at hand. Other people were joining the party, shaking hands, slapping backs, and clinking glasses. The bar was getting more crowded as the newcomers arrived and jockeyed for position to get the bartender's attention.

"So what are you going to do? I mean is there a funeral or something?"

Rex rubbed his forehead again and wished he were alone. Lucy was making him think about things he didn't want to think about.

"Yeah, I don't know. Like I said, I didn't really know her that well. The police are involved and..." Rex cut himself off to change subjects. "Let me see the pictures again. The place is starting to fill up; these guys could already be in here somewhere."

They had their backs to the crowd. Rex focused in on the faces, trying to burn the images into his mind. One of the guys looked like an actor he'd seen somewhere. The guy had a broad forehead, wide-set eyes, and big shoulders. He looked like he might have played football in college.

"Hey, that looks like me."

The voice came from behind them. Rex turned around and looked right into the same face as in the picture.

The guy was already close enough for Rex to smell the acrid aroma of too much cologne. He was wearing khaki slacks, a dress shirt with an open collar, and a sports coat. The jacket was an average blue blazer, the footwear, semi-casual loafers. The clothing seemed thrown together, and Rex thought it was safe to assume that his new friend was, in fact, a military general appearing at this party, out of uniform and maybe struggling to fit into a situation where everybody was not obligated to kiss his ass. Rex couldn't figure out how the guy got behind him and saw the picture but obviously, he was not functioning at his best after absorbing the shocking news. He suddenly felt a bit light headed.

"Is that yours, sport?"

"What? The picture? It was on the bar."

"On the bar."

"Yep, and then I picked it up."

"Right. Except you didn't answer my question."

Rex became aware that two more dudes were shouldering their way through the crowd and now appeared at the first guy's flank. None of them were wearing uniforms—they all had business casual attire that they didn't look completely natural wearing.

"You got more of those pictures, sport?"

"A couple, yeah."

"Can I see those?"

Rex weighed his options. The crowd had thickened up quite a bit and there was no way he could slip out of this situation without having some kind of interaction with the guy standing in front of him. He glanced at Lucy but she just rolled her eyeballs, indicating she had no idea how to help. Two other dudes who resembled guys in the other pictures appeared at the general's side. Rex slowly handed over the Polaroids and took half a step back, planning his exit if he needed to make a break for it.

The other two guys stood behind the general, squinting at the pictures. "What's up, Hap?" one of them said.

The guy named Hap quickly waved the photos at the other guy and said, "Apparently we're some kind of famous." His eyes bored into Rex. "Where'd you get these, sport? Did you take them?"

"No, those are Polaroids. I don't even have one of those cameras. The pictures were laying on the bar when I came up."

"Laying on the bar, huh? Quite a coincidence. So, since they're not yours and since we're in them, you probably won't mind if we just hold onto them?

Hap, the general, opened his jacket and Rex watched his evidence slipping away.

"Wait—they're not mine, but they were given to me, and I think he wants them back."

"Who's he?" said the general.

Rex looked back at him, searching for some kind of truth that would extricate him from the situation without compromising his mission. He felt himself breaking into a sweat – again. He tried to imagine what James Bond would do.

"Can we step outside and talk for a second, sir?"

"Lead the way," said the general.

Rex glanced at Lucy and gave her a quick wave. He wasn't sure if he wanted her to follow him or just acknowledge that he was stepping out of the room with his new friends. He dropped his head and turned toward the nearest door, not bothering to look to see who was following him. He considered making a run for it but didn't want to cause more of a scene than he already was.

He reached the hallway, glanced behind him and walked toward a section where nobody was standing around. Rex turned to face his accusers. Lucy appeared off to the side of the guys with her arms folded.

The general squared his stance like he was getting ready to punch Rex in the face and said, "All right, mister, spill. Who are you, what are you doing here, and how did get the pictures?"

Rex cleared his throat and stole a glance toward Lucy. She shrugged, looked back at Rex and said, "Go ahead, tell him."

Rex took a deep breath and said, "My name is Rex Armstrong. I work for the Federal Development Commission, which is a small independent agency that evaluates GSA-owned buildings. I was recruited by a guy named Wellborn to infiltrate this party, look for the guys in those pictures, and see what they were up to. In short, sir, the guy who hired me told me you guys are generals and that you are suspected of sharing drone technology with the French."

The general didn't move or say a word. His face went blank for a full five seconds. He then burst out laughing so loud that Rex and Lucy both jumped. Composing himself, the general said, "Drone technology? To the French?" Then he laughed even harder and louder. Rex found himself chuckling along with him.

"You got to be fucking kidding me. Seriously? The French are allies, Armstrong. I'm sure you realize that. You are American, aren't you? They gave us the fucking Statue of Liberty, for Chrissakes."

Rex shrugged. "I don't know anything about that, sir. I'm just doing what I was hired to do."

"I see. And who does this Wellborn guy work for?"

"He won't tell me," Rex said.

"Fucking spooks. What's he look like?"

"Very average looking. He's got dark hair and a square face and wears a hat that matches his suit. He's always reading a newspaper, and he talks kind of funny, like a minister or something."

One of the other generals groaned and said, "Goddamit." The other one said, half under his breath, "The priest."

Hap moved closer to Rex and lowered his voice. "If Skip here is right, you're being played by one of the best. The priest has his fingers in a lot of pots and now he's into yours."

"The priest?"

"'Fraid so."

"So if you guys know him, who does he work for?"

"Doesn't matter. He's a firefighter—sort of a contract fixer who works all over town, hunting rats, fighting evildoers, solving problems." Rex was quietly freaking out on the inside about blowing his cover within minutes of being on the job and was sure his career as a spy was over but he squared his jaw and pretended it wasn't bothering him.

Plus, maybe the generals were the good guys. Maybe Wellborn, the priest was the bad guy. Hap smoothed his hair with both hands. "Look, we need to get back to the party before the frogs get jumpy. I'm surprised they aren't out here already asking questions. By the way, these are my colleagues, Skip and Hokey."

"Hap, Skip, and Hokey? Seriously?" Lucy said. "Did you guys just make those names up?"

Hap took two steps toward Lucy and said, "And we still don't know this charming creature's sobriquet."

"My friends call me Lucy, but you can call me, Ms. Wright."

Hap chuckled. "Fair enough, Ms. Wright, fair enough. Let's go get a drink."

Rex stepped over to Lucy and said, "Are you all right?"

"I need a martini. Maybe a double martini, if there is such a thing."

Hap, Rex, and Lucy approached the bar. "I'll have a double bourbon, neat, and please take care of my friends as well," the general said. He pulled a twenty dollar bill off a bankroll that appeared out of his pocket, and stuffed it into the tip jar.

"I'll have what he's having," Lucy said.

"Make it three," Rex said.

The general nodded approval to their drink choices. He pulled a pair of glasses out of his jacket pocket and squinted at the Polaroids one at a time.

"Hmph. No wonder he thinks we're in bed with the froggies."

Rex took a sip of the bourbon and felt the liquor burn its way down. "Why? What are you talking about?"

The general moved the pictures like a fan. The look on his face implied he was thinking hard about whether to reveal any more. He looked down his nose at Lucy and said, "How are you involved in all this, Ms. Wright?"

Lucy drained half her oversize shot. "I'm his neighbor."

Hap laughed again, stopped fanning the images and handed them back to Lucy.

"His neighbor? Jesus, the priest has outdone himself this time, hasn't he? Hiring unsuspecting amateurs and their neighbors to do his grunt work. You getting paid for this, Armstrong?"

"Yes, but maybe not enough."

"Probably not. Probably not. Okay, here's the deal. The pictures were taken at a party, just like this one, over in that corner of the room. One shot of me, one of Hokie, one of Skip, all hanging out with, well, let's just say, hanging out with some guys who, if you were going to sell drone technology to the French, would be the right guys to hang out with. I can see why the priest is suspicious. But the pictures don't prove anything and the fact that we're here tonight doesn't prove anything. In short, you're pumping a dry hole. You're on a goose chase with an empty gun." He finished his bourbon. "And you're currently swimming in the deep end of the pool without the proper supervision."

He motioned for the bartender to refill the glass. "Does the priest know anything about your personal life? Any skeletons in the closet you don't want to see dancing around in the daylight?"

Rex drained his own glass. "I don't know. Maybe."

A tall, good-looking, dark-skinned man suddenly appeared in the space, gliding up to Hap with an outstretched hand. "Good to see you, my friend. Thank you for coming." There was a trace of an accent and there was something familiar about the guy's manner to Rex. Hap shook his hand and gestured toward Rex and Lucy. "Hello, François, nice to see you. These are my friends, Ms. Wright and Mr. Armstrong." François gave them a quick nod and touched Hap's upper arm. "May I speak to you for a moment, sir?"

"Of course," Hap said. "If you two will excuse me. Stay out of trouble, Armstrong, and I mean that."

Rex waved him off, ordered two more bourbons, exhaled and said, "Holy shit."

"Holy shit is right," said Lucy in a rush of breath. "What the hell have you got me into? Are you out of your mind, telling him the whole deal?"

"You said, 'Tell him.'"

"Yeah, but I didn't mean tell him, tell him. I meant tell him something."

Rex held the now refilled bourbon glass to his head like it was a cold compress. Maybe the soothing effects of the alcohol would transfer through the glass into his skull and calm his worried mind. "I have to think for a second. The guy on the phone said the cops are looking for me because they want to question me about the dead girl."

"Wait. What? The cops are looking for you because why?"

"Apparently I was one of the last people to see her alive. And it was the night I blacked out at the club. Something very weird is going on. Come on, let's get out of here."

"Wait, what are you going to tell your contact about what happened here tonight?"

"Why, the truth, of course. What else would I tell him?"

Rex and Lucy made a graceful exit. The generals had mixed into various conversational knots and Rex felt no compunction to say farewell. He walked Lucy to her apartment door, made sure she was okay and kissed her on the cheek. He rode the elevator down to his floor, turned down the hall, and walked right into two guys. They were wearing casual clothes, but one of them was talking into a crackling radio.

"Whoa. Here we go," the dude without the radio said. "Any chance you're Rex Armstrong?"

"Who wants to know?" Rex looked into a wide cheek-boned face. The dude was average height and build with short dark hair. His buddy with the radio was taller and had a triangular face and sleepy eyelids. Both of them pulled badges out of their jackets and flashed them.

"DC Metro PD. Are you Rex Armstrong, sir?" said Cheekbones.

Rex looked them over. "Yes, I am. But I've had a rough night. If this is about the speeding tickets, I already paid them." Rex tried to walk by them but the cheekbones guy caught him by the upper arm and then blocked his path.

"This isn't about speeding tickets, sir. Mind if we step into your place and have a little chat?"

"You got a warrant?"

"We're not here to search your place. We just want to ask you a few questions about a woman you may know," the tall guy said.

"Why do we need to go inside? Just tell me what's on your mind."

The two guys looked at each other and the shorter guy leaned in toward him. "Listen. This is about a possible homicide. If you don't mind sharing your personal business with every neighbor who lives along this hallway…"

"Okay, fine. Come with me, officers." Rex brushed by them, pulling out his keys and letting them in.

Rex pulled a bottle of bourbon off the countertop and poured a generous amount into a glass of ice. "Cocktail, officers?"

"Actually it's detective," Cheekbones said. "I'm Detective Span, and this is my partner, Detective Franklin."

"Okay, Span and Franklin, what can I do for you?"

"Live here by yourself, Mr. Armstrong?" Span asked.

"Yes. Next question."

"Oh, he gets right to the point, doesn't he?" Franklin said.

Span reached into his shirt pocket, pulled out a picture and showed it to Rex. It was Amy. From her position in the photo, it looked like her hands were tied behind her. Her face was bruised, her eyes were closed, her mouth was half open and she was naked from the waist up.

Rex swallowed a big gulp of liquor. "I know her. Her name's Amy."

"Amy what?" Franklin asked.

"I don't know her last name. What happened to her?"

"We were hoping you could tell us, Armstrong," Franklin said. "According to what we know so far, you were one the last two people to see her alive. You go to a sex club out in Montgomery County? Know a guy named Chester Thompson?"

"You already know I do...What does that have anything to do with anything?"

Franklin grimaced like he was trying to keep his cool. "I'll tell you what it has to do with. Our girl Amy here was strangled to death—but not just in your usual strangling death kind of way. She had her arms and legs tied up, with, um, shall we say, some very specialized kinds of rope. The M.E. puts her time of death at a few hours past when you saw her at Chester's pervo club. So assuming you're a member of that fine establishment, I'd like to know if maybe you're missing anything from your toy box and if you'd have any reason to snuff out Ms. Amy. Or maybe it was just some kinky sex scene that got out of hand. Anything you'd like to tell us, Rexy?" Franklin's eyes focused on him like little gray laser beams.

"Aren't you guys supposed to read me my rights or something here?"

"Only if you're under arrest," Span said.

"And am I under arrest?"

"Not yet," Franklin said. "Why, have you done something that would give us a reason to arrest you?"

Rex wiped his hand down his face and said, "Look. I did see her that night, okay? I was walking her out to the car. She wanted to change shoes. I blacked out. Somebody jumped me from behind, I think. Or, I don't know, I may have had a concussion from something that happened earlier in the day. Chester told me that Amy came back into the club. She told him I passed out. When I woke up, she was already gone."

Span made a tooth sucking sound. "And that's it? You didn't go find her or meet up with her later?"

"No. I came home."

"Came home by yourself?" Franklin asked.

"By myself."

"Can anybody confirm that you were home alone?" Span

asked.

"Of course not. I was by myself."

"Yeah," Franklin said. "See, that's the whole problem with that alibi."

"Alibi? It's not an alibi. It's the truth," Rex shot back.

"Yeah, well, the truth is hard to come by sometimes, Mr. Armstrong. Did you see a doctor about this blackout or concussion or attack or whatever it was?" Span asked.

"No."

Span made another tooth sucking sound. "Okay, here's the deal. The boys in the lab are playing with the ropes and some other items found at the scene, so at some point, we may need you to provide DNA samples, fingerprints, that kind of thing, just to rule out your involvement. Are you willing to cooperate with all that?"

"Yes, of course. I didn't kill her, fellas. I was rather fond of her, but I didn't know her that well. Where was she found?"

Span slid the picture back into his pocket. "Potomac. The high rent district."

"See? We're a long way from Potomac down here."

"Obviously. We think the body was actually moved there. She probably died somewhere else. One more thing. I know it sounds like something out of the movies, but if you plan on leaving town, we'd kind of like to know about it. Understand?"

"Sure," Rex said. "I understand."

CHAPTER 8

Rex awoke feeling groggy and uneven from the consumption
and the events of the night before. He upped his caffeine intake by
selecting an extra-large cup from his cabinet at home and then
backed it up with another one from the break room upon reaching
the office. He picked through his federal employee inbox clicking
on the stuff that looked important and deleting the trash.

He started searching the web for "The Priest," already
knowing that he would find nothing. Whoever Wellborn was, he
probably wasn't going to show up on the Internet. He also searched
for any coverage of Amy's death. He wasn't even sure if Amy was
her real name or just her scene name.

He couldn't find anything and wondered if it was being
downplayed or held until they found her next of kin. Rex's boss
was at a conference so there was no pressure to get anything
done—pretty much business as usual. He kept himself busy
resizing images and then left in plenty of time to be on time for
lunch.

Wellborn was at the same table where Rex left him after the
last lunch and was reading the day's *New York Times*. The hat
matching the suit rested on the chair next to him.

"What's the news from Gotham, Commissioner Gordon?"

"Much the same as yesterday, Mr. Armstrong." Wellborn
didn't look up. He snapped the paper closed and said, "So, how did

it go last night—any problems?"

Rex took the chair across from him and said, "I'm afraid so. While my date and I were looking at the pictures, the generals who are in the pictures saw me."

"Oh, you took a date? How interesting. And what did you tell her regarding your purpose for being there?

"I told her the truth, of course—isn't that what you always advise?"

"The truth shall make you free," Wellborn said.

"I'm glad you said that. It's biblical, isn't it?"

"A rough translation from the book of John, eighth chapter, methinks."

Rex dropped the napkin into his lap. "The generals seem to think you are somebody they call the priest."

Wellborn's motions came to a sudden full stop but his expression never changed. Then he laughed out loud, which reverberated through the sparsely occupied restaurant.

"I'm sorry. That always amuses me, especially since I'm not even Catholic." This caused him to start laughing again.

His guffaws eventually subsided into chuckles. He dabbed at the corners of his eyes with his napkin. "Very well, Mr. Armstrong. I have been called that nickname from time to time, and since I have heard of the generals, I'm glad they have heard of me. Now. Down to business, shall we?"

The waiter interrupted them. They placed food orders and then Wellborn continued. "So obviously the generals were there, they saw the Polaroids, you talked to them, and they talked back. Sounds very illuminating. Tell me, did you see them interacting with anybody else who appears in those pictures we gave you?"

"You mean somebody like François?"

"Oh, very well done, Mr. Armstrong. So you met François?"

"I did. Very briefly. And he seems kind of familiar to me—like I've met him before."

"That would not surprise me, Rex. He gets around, that one."

"So, the generals tell me that we're barking up the wrong tree here and that are not selling drone technology to the French."

"Well, what else would they say? You don't expect the U.S. military to tell you the truth, do you?"

"Actually, I do expect that, and Hap didn't seem to be lying."

"Oh, you're on a first-name basis with General Hap Peterson? Well, isn't that just ducky? And so why are they consorting with the unsavory characters they are associating with? Did he explain that to you?"

"No, and maybe you should ask him yourself since you all seem to know each other so well. Why don't you just have lunch with Hap and you boys can straighten all this out? Aren't we all on the same side, here?"

Wellborn held up his butter knife and pointed it Rex's general direction as he scanned the tabletop, "I certainly hope so. Would you be so kind as to pass the butter?"

"Why certainly, your priesthood, but how about explaining what all this has to do with Metro and the missing money and all that hoopla?"

Wellborn gave Rex a look as he digested the "priesthood" reference. He cut into the butter like a surgeon. "Since you want to play connect the dots today, let's say you're a French patriot who wants to buy drone technology so that your client, the French defense industry, can make its own drones and sell them to all the other countries out there who want their very own fleet of flying killer robots. And let's say that since the French people are generally peace-loving anarchists who will go way out of their way to not support any kind of a war effort in other countries, the chance of you getting funds from the French government to purchase said technology is pretty much non-existent. If all this were true, you would need a sum of untraceable cash to buy the secrets, now wouldn't you?

"So, François and his buddies steal money from the Metro, pay the generals, who put them onto whatever they need to build the drones, which the French then sell, and everybody's happy. Is that about it?"

"In a nutshell, that is how it's supposed to work."

"That's kind of fucked-up, isn't it?"

"We certainly think so."

The drinks arrived and Rex slowly sipped his soda while watching Wellborn's studied movements. "So, what's the next step, assuming you want me to keep working on the case?"

"The next step would be for you to see if you can befriend François and find out whatever you can, preferably without sharing your mission with everybody you converse with. You know, for a James Bond in training, you're not keeping a very low profile with your new part-time job."

Rex tore off a piece of crusty bread, poured some olive oil into a shallow bowl and swirled the crust around in it. "Actually, as I recall, James Bond caused stirs wherever he went."

"Touché', Rex. Is this something you want to move forward with?

"Absolutely, assuming the money keeps coming in."

"Oh, I'm glad you reminded me." Wellborn pulled an envelope out of his jacket pocket and handed it to Rex. "I believe that evens us up."

"You know, if I keep bringing Lucy along you may have to hire her, too."

"That's not likely. We've hired you. If you want to hire

someone to act as your date, those funds would, as they say, 'come out of your end.'"

Rex slipped the envelope into his pocket and said, "Fine, fine, fine. So how do I find François so I can make him my new best friend?"

"Well, as luck would have it, we know he frequents a certain fetish club in town—remember we were discussing this before?"

"Sure, I remember." Rex's mind began flashing through the set of aliases and faces that he knew from the scene. He knew François looked familiar—maybe he'd seen him at one of the parties.

"Which club?"

"There's a business card in the envelope with the cash. Have a look when you're somewhere private. See if you can arrange to run into the person of interest so it doesn't look too suspicious and let us know what you find. Pretty simple, really, and it's good for another cash installment."

"Any chance we can raise the rate, again? I have a little tax problem I'm trying to take care of."

"Also highly unlikely, especially if you keep as they say, 'blowing your cover.'"

The food arrived and the two men worked their way through the meal as the conversation ratcheted down to small talk about sports, politics, and the weather. Rex offered to pick up the tab but Wellborn refused. He said farewell to his handler and went back to the office feeling pretty good about things until the unpleasant memory of Amy and the Metro cops came crashing back through his skull. He slumped back into his chair and texted Lucy.

"How are you feeling today, young lady?"

"Like I was run over by a whiskey train. Leave me out of your next adventure."

Rex texted her a frowny-face emoji in response, opened the

envelope, counted the crisper-than-real bills, and pulled out the business card. Big surprise—it came from Chester's club. Right on cue, Rex got a text from Chester asking him if he was planning to attend the weekly BDSM Happy Hour that evening. Rex usually steered clear of theses things, as they were full of self-involved millennials, swingers he didn't want to swing with, and desperate dudes feigning kinky in the hopes of an easy hookup. Rex assured Chester he would meet him there so they could compare notes on the recent happenings. And so the evening plans were laid.

CHAPTER 9

Rex suited up by dressing in black and rubbed some product into his hair. Happy hours and "munches" were the low-stress meet and greet tools used in the scene to indoctrinate new recruits, keep tabs on upcoming events and hunt for fresh meat. Being older, more established and not needing to impress anybody, Rex avoided them like the plague, preferring private events where there would actually be some action.

The venue was a dive bar on Connecticut Avenue, south of Dupont Circle. The joint was carved out of a basement space and outfitted with a big screen TV, crappy, second-hand bar furniture, a small performance space at the far end, and low lighting. Rex rode the motorcycle, found parking out front, passed the look-over test from the guy working the door and headed to the bar. Chester was already in place, with a 20-something wearing too much eye makeup perched on his lap.

"Making yourself at home, I see," Rex said.

"Just trying to lend my years of experience to the younger generation, my friend."

Chester lifted the girl to her feet. "Give us a moment, will you, love? Guy talk. I'll rejoin you in a moment." The chick made a face of rejection mixed with slight irritation, stood up and teetered away on heels that looked like they were way too high.

"I wanna be you when I grow up," Rex said. "Can I buy you a

drink?”

“Why, certainly. Feeling flush, are we?”

“Well, let’s say I’ve opened up a new income stream.”

“Always good to hear, Reximus. So, have the local authorities paid you a visit yet?”

“As a matter of fact they I have, and I implicated you.”

A look of semi-real horror shot over Chester’s round face, as Rex slapped him on the shoulder and said, “I’m kidding, of course. The whole thing is fucked up. They actually told me to not leave town—I’m the prime suspect.”

“Yeah, well better than you than me, mate. She had one of my business cards on her, so they were keen to talk to me.”

Rex ordered a bourbon and motioned to the bartender to get Chester a fresh one as well. “Speaking of which, have you ever seen any of these guys?” Rex pulled one of the Polaroids out of his pocket and slipped it across the bar.

“Polaroids? Hmmm… You know there’s a fetish for these.”

“And I’m sure you would know all about it. Look at the guys, Chester—do you know any of these schmos?”

“Not a very attractive bunch, are they? I do know the dark-skinned chap who seems to be skulking around in the shadows.” Chester laid the picture on the bar and turned back to his drink.

“And?”

“And what, Rex? You know I can’t be blabbing about people in the scene to other people in the scene, especially with this nasty bit of business going on. Where did you get those pictures, anyway? What are you onto, Rex, old boy? Playing private dick or something?”

“Something like that. Look, I don’t need to know his address and credit card number, just tell me what you know. I promise not to reveal whatever you're about to reveal."

Chester studied Rex's face for several seconds, looked over his shoulder and said, "Okay, but don't repeat any of this as I will deny everything. His name is François. Not sure if that's his scene name or real name. I think he's French Canadian, or maybe Czech or something. He's a common, garden-variety Dom, likes rope bondage, some impact play, and enjoys long walks on the beach. Turns up at the club occasionally and…"

"And what?"

Chester took a long drink from his glass and said, "And I've seen him with Amy. Or did see him with Amy, you know, before she, you know."

"What?"

"Yeah, they were pretty hot and heavy for awhile I think."

"No shit."

"No shit. So what's it all about then, Rex? What's the story behind the story?

Rex tapped the edge of the Polaroid against the bar and said, "I don't know, but it may have something to do with a plan to rip off the Metro system."

"Rip off the Metro? HA! Well, that all makes perfect sense then, doesn't it?"

"How so?"

Chester brought his face down close to Rex and said, "You don't know? What Amy did in real life?" Rex shook his head as Chester brought his face even closer to Rex and said, "She worked for Metro. Comptrollers' office or something like that."

"No shit."

"I shit you not. Now if you will excuse me, I need to find my date and make it all better." Chester hauled himself off the barstool but then turned to Rex and said, "Oh, by the way, there's a Shibari workshop on Saturday night at the club. I would expect that person that you're interested in will probably be there."

"Shibari? The intricate rope bondage stuff?"

"Indeed sir. Japanese style. Very devilish stuff. Leaves very interesting marks, don't you know."

Rex had been to a couple of rope bondage workshops and learned some of the basics but at some point, he decided he didn't usually have the patience for the ritual that went with it.

He waved off Chester, looked at his reflection in the mirror and said, "Hmmm, I would need a partner to go to something like that. I wonder who I could ask?" He looked around the bar for a familiar face. He downed the drink, briefly considered ordering a second but changed his mind and headed out. He got back home and was relieved to see that there weren't any policeman lurking about in his hallway. He googled "shibari," and texted Lucy.

"Do you have any plans for Saturday night?"

"Planning on making new friends in the US military?"

"Have you ever been tied up?"

"Shirley, you must be joking. Call me tomorrow, I'm asleep."

Rex smiled and texted her an emoticon of a devil's head. He texted Wellborn, saying he had a lead on François. Then he went to bed and fell into a deep, dreamless sleep.

CHAPTER 10

The workweek returned in a gray blur of mindless tasks. Rex debated sending the IRS a check but was afraid that if he started sending them money they would sink their talons deeper into his flesh and finances. He put in a call to his CPA, seeking advice. Just as he hung up, his phone rang back. Shocked by the quick response from the accountant he checked the screen and saw it was Lucy.

"I thought I was calling you," he said.

"Yeah, well, it's your lucky day, big boy. What the hell did that text mean last night? What's going on?"

"The guy that came up to the generals at the party we attended is a person of interest to the Feds and also the DC police department. He may have been the one who killed my friend from the club. I need to go out to the club on Saturday and see what I can find out but I need a, um, rope bunny."

"Rope bunny? Rex, have you considered getting professional help for this double life you're leading? I mean, it's got its own language, a separate set of rules…maybe you should try being normal for a while. Watch some TV, go to a ball game or something. Isn't that what normal guys do?"

"I don't know what normal guys do because I'm not a normal guy. Listen, the only rope chick I know was Amy, and she is no longer available. Do me a favor and go with me. There's usually no nudity and all you have to do is stand there and get tied up. You might even enjoy the experience. A lot of people do." There were several seconds of silence and Rex assumed the call was dropped.

He pulled the phone away from his ear and could see that she was still on the line.

"Hello?" he said.

"Do they sell drinks there?"

"Ummm, no. Not on bondage nights. It violates some kind of liquor laws."

"Again with the crazy rules."

"Listen. We can take a flask, as long as we keep it out of sight. They're very tame, these things. It's called shibari and it's all about the way the knots look—almost like an art project. I promise you won't have to do anything that makes you uncomfortable."

"But I will be tied up. You think that might make me uncomfortable? What if I decide, all of a sudden like, that I don't want to be tied up anymore?"

"Every rigger keeps a very sharp knife in their bag. If someone starts to freak out, they just cut the ropes."

"That doesn't really help me, Rex. Who are these people who go to these things? It just sounds totally creepy to me."

Rex said nothing, again waiting like the car salesman. This time he forced himself not to talk hoping her curiosity would overpower her dread.

"Call me on Saturday and I'll let you know," said Lucy. My cousin may be in town and I'm not sure she would want to be part of this. I gotta go. Talk to you later."

Rex was hopeful. He muddled through the rest of the week weighing his options. Every time he heard voices in his hallway he got nervous, thinking it might be the cops with new, incriminating piece of evidence against him for a crime he didn't commit. At home, he researched shibari, trying to give himself a better knowledge of the knots and tying system.

Rex never had the desire to be a hardcore rope rigger. He

knew some of the basic knots from Boy Scouts. Who knew those merit badges would come in handy for something like this? A lot of the rope guys weren't in it for the sex. For them, it was more about working with the ropes, perfecting the knots, and in some cases watching the victims struggle to escape. Rex felt that if he was going to go to all the trouble of tying women up then he wanted to have sex with them.

He surfed the popular bondage sites, flipping through discussions about rope type, length, color, and favorite positions. There were warnings about nerve damage from tying somebody too tight, and more dire words about leaving a bound person alone while tied. He flipped over to Chester's site and read the write-up about the workshop. It was being taught by a muckety-muck from the rope world and would cost Rex $50 to play. There was a long detailed list of suggested rope lengths to bring.

"Jesus, how many people are we tying?" Rex thought. He went to his toy box, pulled out all the rope he had and realized he was a lousy rope guy. His collection included odd lengths, different colors, and different diameters, which marked him as a bona fide amateur. He considered a trip to Home Depot, but most of their stuff had nylon in it, which you weren't supposed to use on people. There was clothesline, which some people swore by. It was cotton and cheap, and usually came in the acceptable colors of white or grey. Using clothesline would work but it would still identify him a beginner, which could limit his chance to befriend François.

He could buy rope online, but that would take too long, and Rex wasn't exactly sure what he really needed other than the suggested lengths. "Looks like we're heading toward the Passion Pit, headquarters for all your kinky needs. Why are there no decent rope shops locally with all the weirdoes we have in this town?" he said to himself. He went out for a final smoke and fell asleep anticipating the events to come.

On Friday evening Rex found himself in a familiar place, the best kinky store in the Washington area, which was actually in Baltimore. It was run by two gay guys who lived upstairs and ran the store downstairs. The building was squat and brick, sitting just on the edge of the Mt. Vernon neighborhood, home to the various upwardly mobile deviants and freaks that supported the enterprise.

The guys made their own impact toys, a fine selection of wooden paddles and leather floggers – including the one Lola had at the club. There were dildos and vibrators, harnesses, boots and shoes, collars, cuffs, quirts – a kind of short-handled riding whip, and full-length single tail whips. There were racks of latex clothing, risqué greeting cards and raunchy novelty items for bachelor and bachelorette parties. Classical music was playing, providing a sheen of high class over the prurient product lines.

Rex walked in and caught a glimpse of one of the owners hammering studs into a leather vest in the back workroom, while the other one, Matt, the slighter and more effeminate of the two, was on the sales floor organizing a rack of specialized video titles. Rex knew his name from other purchases and conversations.

"I need help," Rex said. "Rope help."

Matt fanned the fingers of one hand over his chest and said, "Talk to me."

"I'm going to a rope bondage workshop tomorrow and I need four fifteens, two thirties, and two sixties."

"You're teaching the workshop?"

"No, attending."

"Seems like a lot of rope."

"That's what I was thinking."

"What diameter?"

"See? That's where I need help. It didn't specify."

"Right. So is it damsel in distress stuff or…"

"Shibari."

"Oh, nice. Come right over here."

Matt led Rex through the shop to the back corner, talking as he was walking. "So shibari is Japanese style, lots of history there. Supposedly the samurai used it on their prisoners, but they called it something else."

"Hojo-jutsu," Rex said.

"Right. That's it. So you do know something about this stuff."

"Well, I've been on the internet."

Matt grabbed the end of a black line on a wooden spool and pulled some off. "Now see, this is a six millimeter, cotton and obviously it's black. Smooth to the touch, washable and fairly inexpensive. A lot of the guys like hemp, which is a bit rougher. I guess it kind of depends on what your model likes, too."

"She's totally vanilla."

"Really? And you're going to use shibari on her? Then I would definitely go with the cotton. Much smoother."

Rex took the line from Matt, ran it through his fingers, and coiled it around his hand while imagining turning it around Lucy's arms and legs. No way she was going to see yes to this. He was going to end up with a shitload of rope and no date for this fiasco. Just then his phone rang. Rex smiled to see that it was Lucy.

"Hello, my darling."

"What are you doing, Rex? I'm going to the bar. Want to join me?"

"I'm shopping right now at a sweet little boutique in Baltimore. Do you look good in black?"

"I look good in everything. Come on over, I think you owe me a drink, or maybe seven."

"I'll be there in an hour or so. What about this thing tomorrow? Can you go with me? I'm kind of in a jam here."

"We can talk about that when you get here. Hurry up."

The line went dead as Rex looked at Matt and said, "What the hell. I'll take it."

Matt repeated the order back and then did a fine job of measuring, sorting, and sealing the ends of the lengths. They stepped toward the cash register. Rex looked down into the glass display case of cock rings, d-rings, and other assorted metalwork.

"I bought one of those the last time I was in here," Rex said. "Still haven't used it."

"What? One of the steel cock rings?"

"Yeah, the chick who requested it kind of disappeared on me."

Matt shrugged and carefully folded the rope into one the store's large purple shopping bags. "Well, that happens sometimes, doesn't it?"

"Yeah. Do you guys make those here?"

"We do," said Matt as he pulled one out of the case, "and as you can see we put our logo on them. Stamp it right in there so everybody knows where the good stuff comes from."

Rex squinted at the heavy steel ring and sure enough, the double, interlocking P's of the Passion Pit were right there.

"That's weird. You know I haven't seen that thing in a while. I wonder where it got to."

Matt had already tuned out, put the ring back in its case, rang up the purchase and smiled to Rex while holding the bag up for him. "Enjoy!"

Rex dropped the shopping bag into a saddlebag, fired up the bike and started the drive back from Baltimore. The grey strip of I-95, the white lines, and the wind began to hypnotize him and his mind wandered. He thought about what it would feel like to put Lucy's arms behind her back and secure her into a helpless state. He tugged at his jeans imagining her squirming and perhaps making wisecracks as he went.

He wondered if she would object to some casual groping and considered that this workshop thing might break down the barriers of their friendship and move their acquaintance into something more intimate. The other risk was that once she saw him in his kinked-up, sleazy little world of perverts, she would never think of him in the same way.

François and the DC Metro Police Department presented a more pressing matter. If there was no way to establish that he hadn't killed Amy, he could be caught up in a nightmare of legal problems that would make the tax problems look like parking tickets.

He wondered how he would make acquaintance with François in between paying attention to the workshop leader and tying up Lucy in a way that didn't jeopardize his relationship with her. Plus, they'd all seen each other at the French party. How was he going to explain that one?

The motorcycle seemed to know its way to the bar. Rex pulled up to the curb, killed the engine, and flipped the kickstand down. The purple shopping bag stayed hidden in the saddlebag. He pulled his helmet off, ruffled his hair, and went inside. Lucy was stationed on the corner stool having a spirited discussion with Joe, the bartender, as Rex approached. He ordered a beer.

"I hate these fucking Yelpers," Joe was saying. "It's like don't they have anything better to do with their life than timing how long it takes to get a pizza, or putting a thermometer in their beer to see how cold it is, and then complaining about their findings. Who are these people?"

Lucy gave Rex a quick hug. "Ever Yelp, Rex? Have any opinions on this?"

Rex grabbed the beer that Joe slid in front of him. "Bunch of wankers, aren't they? Freelance food critics without an actual paying platform, so they take it out on poor fuckers like Joe here."

"Exactly," said Joe. "How would they like it if I came to their place of business and critiqued their job performance?"

"But you work in the public eye, Joe," Lucy said. "You must be held accountable to the whims and taste of the public. Your job and your very existence depend on making these so-called wankers, being made happy wankers."

"Agreed," Joe said. "But some of these so-called wankers will never be happy with anything. They go into a place with a chip on their shoulder, looking for a bad time, and then they get exactly what they're expecting."

Joe was called away to serve another customer. Rex looked at Lucy, imagining her tied up, her torso bisected into a weave of lines encircling her breasts, stretching around her belly. And he thought about her suspended in a black cotton rope harness.

"What are you thinking about, Rex? Looks like you have evil on your mind."

"Nothing. How did you guys get into this whole Yelp conversation?"

"Oh, the bar got a bad review from some bridge-and-tunnel-crowd douchebag and so Joe heard about it from the owner."

"'Bridge-and-tunnel-crowd douchebag.' That's very funny. Can I steal that line? You really are quite clever, aren't you, Ms. Wright?"

"Mmm-hmm. Listen. Rex. I can't do that thing tomorrow. My cousin isn't coming but, I don't know, it just sounds too weird for me. I have enough problems without getting any deeper into this wacky shit that you're mixed up in. I mean. I'm crazy about you, you know that. You're like my best guy friend I've ever had. Are you going to hate me if I say no?"

Rex felt his heart sinking and the back of his neck heat up with anxiety, but he couldn't hate Lucy. Not while he was sitting here looking at her.

"No. I won't hate you. I have mixed feelings about it myself. I'm afraid it will fuck up the friendship, too, and I understand why you're hesitant. I don't how I got into this situation with the dead girl, the cops and the spies, so deep, so fast. My lousy temper, I reckon." He took a big swig from the beer and looked away from her, trying to lighten the tension now strung between them.

The bar was loud and crowded. He considered walking up to one of the young, well-scrubbed Capitol Hill staffers and saying something like, "Excuse me, young lady, my name is Rex Armstrong and I'm a murder suspect. Any chance you would like to go on a date tomorrow to a fetish club, where you'll be tied up?" He was an idiot and deserved to be in the situation he was currently wallowing around in.

"You're telling me with all these kinky folks you know you can't find somebody to be your stand-in rope bunny?" Lucy asked. Rex considered the possibility of putting a blurb on the electronic bulletin board that all the area kinksters subscribed to and knew she had a point. He probably could get some bimbo who was otherwise unoccupied on Saturday night to show up and participate but he was hoping to get somebody he knew and liked. Somebody like his friend Lucy.

"Yes, I can do that. Don't worry about it, Luce. The whole thing is so far-fetched anyway, I can't believe it's even real. Let's get some shots and talk about something else." Rex ordered up some bourbon and steered the conversation into safer waters. They talked about his boring job, her boring job, baseball, politics, and the weird state of life they were both occupying in the District of Columbia. Alleged grownups acting like kids with the bar standing in for the playground and cafeteria rolled into one. The minutes stretched into hours, the shots kept coming as Joe came back, checked in, and re-supplied their inebriated joy.

At some point, after midnight they agreed they'd had enough. They split the tab, swayed through the double doors, arm and arm out onto First Street and picked their way down the sidewalk, already lamenting how bad they would feel the next day.

A black, four-door sedan with dinner plate-sized wheel covers glided by them as Rex said, "oh look, there goes some cops pretending not to be cops and hoping that nobody notices. It's a good thing we're not driving, we'd be arrested for sure."

"Is there such a thing as 'walking while under the influence?" asked Lucy who laughed at her own joke while the sedan nudged against the curb ahead of them and doors popped open.

Rex felt a wave of recognition and then shock as the familiar faces of detectives Span and Franklin came into clear focus.

"Oh, fuck," Rex said.

"What?"

"Shhh. I know these guys. Let me do the talking."

The two cops stood on the sidewalk blocking their path. "Out for a evening stroll, Mr. Armstrong?" Franklin asked.

"Just heading home after dinner, gentlemen. Any law against that?"

"Not at all, Rex. As long as you're not showing signs of being intoxicated in public. Aren't you going to introduce us to your dining companion?"

"Well, sure. Detectives Span and Franklin, this is Ms. Lucy. Say hi to the coppers, Ms. Lucy."

"That your first name or last name, Ms. Lucy?" Franklin asked.

"What is this, an interrogation or something?" Rex snapped.

"No, Rex. We're just talking, that's all," Span finally spoke up, holding his hands up and staying in his role as the good cop. "Any chance we can speak to you privately for a moment. There's something we want you to look at."

"I don't want to see any more hinky pictures of Amy, so if that's what's on your mind, the answer is no."

"Who's Amy?" Lucy asked.

"Oh, Ms. Lucy speaks," Franklin said. "Amy is the girl who was killed last week—your escort here was one of the last people to see her alive. Or hasn't he told you that story yet?" Franklin said.

Span shot Franklin a look. "Easy, Don."

Rex took a step toward both of them and said, "Yeah, go real easy, Don. Unless you're going to formally accuse me of something, I don't like the tone."

Franklin slowly reached inside his jacket. "You don't have to like it Rex, and you don't have to look at what I want to show you, but it might be of interest to you." Rex watched his hand and expected to see a pistol come out or maybe a sap, but instead, it was a zip lock baggie—and inside the baggie was a steel cock ring that looked exactly like the one Rex had just noticed he was missing. He felt himself swallow involuntarily and knew as a soon as he did it that cops noticed.

"Does this look familiar to you, Rex? Any chance you're missing one of these?"

Even through the folds of the baggie and in the uneven light coming down from the streetlamps, Rex could make out the double P logo of the Passion Pit.

"Gee, I don't know fellas. What is it? Something you tie your dog to when you're done kicking it?"

Franklin lowered the bag and said, "Did you hear that, detective? I believe Mr. Armstrong is trying to insult us. I believe he may be intoxicated. Maybe a field test is in order to see if these two are a menace to the public. He may be the guy we saw a block over urinating on a federal building. That's a crime, isn't it?"

Rex felt his arm sliding off Lucy's shoulder. He reset his feet, hoping to get a better angle for punching Detective Franklin right in the face. Time slowed. He took a deep breath, picking out the spot on Franklin's nose where he wanted to land the punch. If he caught him squarely, he could then pivot and push Span off his feet. Then he and Lucy would make a run…. He felt Lucy grabbing his arm and pulling it back into position around her shoulders.

She said, "Look, fellas. We don't want any trouble. I don't know anything about Amy, but I do know Rex, and he's a good, upstanding dude. I've had too much to drink and he was just making sure I got home safely. We live right across the street. So, if we can just be on our way, we'll be home in two shakes and won't be a menace to anybody. So, can we just say goodnight?"

"Ms. Lucy speaks as the voice of reason. Did you hear that, Detective Span?" Franklin said. "She's making a lot of sense for an intoxicated person, isn't she? Maybe Rex is the only one who's drunk. Maybe he's the only one who needs to go to jail."

Rex gathered himself, pushing the anger away and surprising himself when he actually felt it move and his judgment clear.

"Okay, I know this is going to sound crazy, but I may actually have a suspect for you—a better suspect then me. It's a guy who knew her, knew her better than me. A guy who is in that scene we were talking about, and a guy she used to sleep with, okay?"

"A very promising lead indeed. What's the gentleman's name? The suspect who's better than you?" said Franklin.

"It may be François. I think he's French. I don't know his last name but I think I can find out for you. Don't take me to jail. I'm supposed to see him tomorrow night."

"Would you be open to having us tag along with you so we can perhaps ask François a few questions? This is serious business and I think the police are in better position to handle it than you are. This is your life we're talking about. Use your head," said Span.

"Believe me, I don't want to be having this conversation with you guys. But I don't even know the guy's last name or even if François is his real first name. Everybody uses aliases in this stuff. Give me the weekend. I'm not leaving town, I'm not going anywhere, I have a job here and I live across the street. Let me get you his real name and I'll turn it all over to you, okay? And you can show him your steel rings and pictures of dead girls and I can get back to my life, okay? Is that a deal?"

Span and Franklin looked at each other as some kind of unseen communication flashed between them while Rex stood on the sidewalk, waiting for an answer that would decide his fate. Rex swallowed hard and remembered the night he went to jail for drunk driving. No sleep, grilled cheese sandwiches and small cartons of milk for breakfast at 6 AM. But the worst part was the feeling of utter worthlessness and guilt. There was no way he could do that tonight. He would try to run away before he let them put him in the squad car. Franklin put the baggie back in his pocket as he stepped toward Rex.

"Here's the deal, Rex. They pulled a partial print off this thing, okay? If that print belongs to you, you got some serious problems. I mean like, call a lawyer kind of problems. You with me? I don't give a shit what people do in their spare time to get their rocks off. It's a free country, right? But I also got a dead blonde white girl in the morgue and right now, you are a live wire leading straight to where all this shit started. So, sure. Take the weekend. Find the mysterious Frenchman and put us onto him. Otherwise, we got to take you in. Understand?"

"Sure," Rex said. "I understand."

Span pulled a business card out of his pocket and handed it to Rex. "So we'll hear from you early next week, right?"

"Yes, early next week," Rex said. He took the card and stood still as they turned, walked back to car and pulled away from the curb. His head began swimming and he felt his guts turning. He pulled away from Lucy, stumbled toward the line of bushes lining the office building they were standing in front of, bent over from the waist and threw-up. He felt Lucy helping him to his feet and pushing a Kleenex into his hand, "Jesus, Rex. What the hell have you gotten yourself into?"

"I'm being framed, Lucy. This is all fucking bullshit. You do believe me, don't you?"

Lucy took his head between her hands and held his face to hers, looking into his watery eyes. "Yes, Rex. I believe you. And I'll go with you tomorrow if it will help you straighten this out."

Then she kissed him on the mouth, the taste of her sweet lip gloss mixing with the acrid bile from the vomit. He woke up the next day stiff, sore and alone.

CHAPTER 11

Rex jumpstarted his brain with a winning combination of drinking caffeine, showering and jamming food down his gullet. He realized that Wellborn hadn't paid him in advance for this gig—which was okay since he seemed to be good for coming up with the dough—but he needed some backup and direction. He texted the spook and asked if he could meet for a chat and strategy session. Wellborn offered to meet him at a park on Capitol Hill at 2:00. Then Rex texted Lucy, thanking her for her faith in him. He told her he would pick her up at seven for the workshop.

He puttered around the apartment, Googled "General Hap Patterson" and found some mentions of him in the military newspapers and defense contractor press releases. There was nothing about drone technology. Was that on purpose? Classified? At the appointed hour he walked toward the park. When he arrived the only people he saw were moms and dads with kids or dogs doing summer in the park things. He walked around the perimeter of the park trying not to look suspicious and scouting for the cat in the hat. The Priest. The priest of what?

Rex walked toward the northeast corner of the park, an area where there was jungle gym equipment set up and an odd-looking trailer. It was beige and windowless and was sitting next to a running portable generator. The door of the trailer opened and Wellborn came out, wearing the traditional hat matching the suit, and closed the door behind him.

"Hello, Rex. Beautiful day in the city, isn't it?"

"If you say so, Wellborn. What is this, your satellite office?"

Wellborn waved his fingers in the air. "Something like that. Just a little temporary space where we can keep an eye on what's happening underground."

"Underground?" Rex looked closer and now saw that the giant air vents of the Metro ran along the sidewalks on both sides of the street. "Oh, I get it. The Metro runs under here. What is it, the Blue line?"

"That's right. You can't believe how many holes there are in the Metro system for bad guys. Ventilation shafts, large electrical conduits, water drains, all kinds of potential disaster. A little explosion here, a little sarin gas there, and it's total pandemonium. Now, what did you want to talk about? I have cash if that's your concern."

They walked along the sidewalk, with Wellborn's hands clasped behind his back. Rex noticed that he had a bit of stoop going in his shoulders and Rex wondered how old he was. "Well, naturally I'll take the cash but I got a bigger problem. The DC Metro Police are asking me about this girl who got killed last week since I was one of the last people to see her alive. I appear to be their prime suspect. But my sources say this François guy that you are interested in knew Amy, the dead girl—knew her in the biblical sense if you'll excuse the reference."

"Well, that's perfect. You are in a position to kill two birds with the same rock. I don't see a downside here."

"The downside is that the DC cops have given me the weekend to bring them something or they're going to put my ass in jail."

"Oh, that wouldn't be good, would it?"

"Not good for me. Not good for you."

"Understood. How can I help?"

"I need François's last name and address so I can hand that to the cops. They go after him, they forget about me, see?"

"Hmmm…assuming François is actually involved. But we're talking murder here? That's really out of his wheelhouse, Rex. I think you may be leading yourself astray, and, besides that, I don't know François's last name or his address. All I have is the pictures and some sketchy background info. It's your job to, as they say, get the lowdown."

"Yeah, well, that's fine. I'm supposed to see him tonight but what I am supposed to do? Go up to the guy and say, 'Hey, buddy what's your real name, what did you do to Amy, and why are you talking to our generals about drone technology?'"

Wellborn stopped, reached into his jacket pocket and pulled out an envelope. "It certainly seems like you have your work cut out for you, Mr. Armstrong. I can't tell you how to do your job but I can tell you most men will talk to a pretty girl and tell her all kinds of things if he's trying to impress her, if you catch my drift. Many people walking this earth are trying to prove things to other people. They're trying to prove they are smarter, richer, faster, more powerful than a locomotive, whatever it is. I would hazard a guess that your new best friend François is just such a person. Take it for what's it's worth and call it my intuition."

Rex took the envelope from Wellborn and folded it into his pocket. "Okay but just in case you're wrong, any possibility you'll bail me out of DC jail? I mean, I'm not sure I'm really cut out for this stuff. I'm in deep shit here. Explain to me again why you recruited me for this?"

Wellborn cocked his head like a dog hearing a funny noise and said, "Do you recall the circumstances on the day we met?"

"Sure. I was getting the shit beat out of me by some security assholes for taking pictures of a building."

"Yes. Bit of a rule breaker, aren't you?"

"Well, yeah, if it's a stupid rule."

"And not afraid of putting yourself in physical danger for a cause that you believe in, yes?"

"Yeah, but I wouldn't call what I was doing a cause."

"Right. Just doing your job, correct?"

"Exactly. Just trying to do my job."

"And so now, we've given you a new job that puts your natural proclivities to work for the forces of good. You are a bit dramatic, but I feel we've made a good choice. In parting I say, Godspeed and good luck, I must get back to my version of crime fighting. Are you heading this way or that?" Rex motioned in the opposite way that Wellborn was facing. "Very well then, Mr. Armstrong. Tally ho."

Rex went home, took a nap and made preparations for the evening and realized he'd never talked to Lucy about their mode of transportation for the evening. He had an aging Mercedes in the parking garage of his building but he usually preferred to ride the motorcycle to events like this. Lucy had never sat on the rear end of his bike. He sent her a text,

"How do you feel about motorcycles?"

"As in riding them?"

"Well, I'm certainly not going to let you drive it."

"Please don't kill me before you tie me up."

"HA! You need to wear boots that protect your ankles."

"Done. See you later."

CHAPTER 12

Lucy was wearing tight black jeans that looked like they had some spandex woven into the fabric to make them form fitting and flattering. For the appropriate amount of ankle protection she'd chosen a pair of tall equestrian-style leather boots in black leather and her top was a high-necked, bare-armed number that also complimented her curves. Rex gulped hard when he saw her come out of the building. He was soon enjoying the feeling of her arms encircling his waist as they rode the bike to the club.

They entered the purposely non-descript doorway and made their way down the darkened hallway, where Rex flashed his club ID to gain access. Rex carried his new rope supply in a black duffle as they approached a circle of five other couples. He felt his heart skip a beat as he noticed that three of the women were already naked.

"Uh-oh."

"What?"

"Some of the rope bunnies have lost their clothes."

"What?! I thought you said…"

"Shh, let me handle this."

Rex approached the leader of the workshop, a longhaired,

bearded, leather-pants-clad dude who called himself, "Sydex," and introduced himself.

"Look, we're kind of new at this and my bottom isn't completely onboard with the nudity—is that an issue?" asked Rex.

Sydex folded his arms across his chest, assuming a defensive posture. "Meaning she herself doesn't want to strip down or she has an issue with the others being nude?"

"Oh, no, she doesn't care about the others, but she's shy and may not want to, you know, get naked."

Sydex looked at Lucy, who was standing off to the side looking everywhere other than toward the semicircle of ropers around her. "Too bad," he said. "Looks like she's in great shape. But no, what she wears is up to her. Just keep in mind that a lot of the ties we're going to be doing are pretty demanding, so the more flexibility she can access, the better. Who knows, once we start she might loosen up and surprise us both."

Rex laughed nervously, nodded and walked back to Lucy. "Okay, you don't have to strip. I swear, the last time I did one of these, everybody was fully clothed."

"Yeah, well some of these ladies would do better to leave some things on, know what I mean?"

"Yes, I do." Rex began pulling the sections of rope out of the duffle and organizing them according to length. "Do you see that guy from the other night, the guy who was talking to the generals?"

"No. I'm not even sure I remember what he looked like. Are you sure there's no bar in here?"

"There is a bar in the back room, but I don't think they sell booze on bondage nights."

"Oh, I see it. I'm going to see if you're wrong about that, too—be right back."

Rex pretended to be fiddling with the ropes while he stole glances at the rest of the participants, hoping that François would be among them. Rex counted the three naked bunnies, another one wearing an oversized t-shirt that she was probably going to take off once things got underway, and another one fully clothed in jeans and a black top. He saw four would-be ropers, all of them sporting elements of standard scene costuming, which included tattoos, chains, studs, body jewelry, piercings, nerdy glasses, and unusual haircuts. That left one Dom missing.

Rex heard the sounds of a conversation approaching. He turned his head to see Lucy walking toward him talking to François who was wearing black, Euro-style jeans, black suede loafers, and a black silk shirt. No visible tattoos, no chains, no jewelry, except for a tasteful silver necklace that encircled his perfectly tanned neckline.

"Look who I found at the bar—which, by the way, is open, Rex. Here's our friend François from the other night at that French thing we went to," Lucy said as she handed Rex a drink.

"Holy shit." Rex stood up. "What are the chances of running into you here?"

"It's a very small town, monsieur. Your date is quite lovely. I'd like to play with her sometime if she has your permission?"

Rex laughed and pulled Lucy closer to him. "Well, we'll see about that, mon ami. Who's your subby tonight?"

François pointed toward two girls talking to each other, both trying to look nonchalant about being naked in public and not doing a completely convincing job of it. "See the small girl, the petite blonde? My regular partner is unavailable, so I'm going to be restraining this little blondie over here. She has the physique of a gymnast, no? Well, see you in a bit." François flashed a dazzling smile at Lucy, gave Rex a quick handshake and walked away.

"Yeah, his regular partner is unavailable because he probably offed her," Rex said half under his breath.

"Am I going to be the only one wearing clothes, Rex?"

"Huh? No. At least I don't think so. How did you meet him? What did you say to him?"

"Oh, not much. He did most of the talking, and he's rather charming. What does all that mean, he wants to 'play' with me if I have 'your permission'? All these hidden meanings—it's all very weird to me."

"Yeah, well, it means he'd like to tie you up—not necessarily have sex with you—but would only do it if I, as your Dom, granted permission, for you as my sub to play with other Doms. Don't worry about it; I would never let you play with him."

"Oh, I won't, Rex, especially since I stopped asking people for permission to play about thirty years ago. Do you think I should take my top off? It's not really that warm in here."

"Wait. What? Jesus, Lucy, leave your top on, for god's sake. We're here to gather information, remember?"

"Oh, I remember fine, and I've already paved the way for you, sir Rex. And what are you saying, you don't want to see me topless? My girls are just as good as all the rest of these ladies— maybe a bit better in some respects. You're not embarrassed by me, are you, sir Rex?"

Rex stood up, ran his fingers through his hair, and took a deep breath. "No, of course, I'm not embarrassed. Your breasts are excellent, from what I've seen, and if you want to take your top off, go right ahead. But I don't want you to feel any more uncomfortable than you already do, that's all. And the correct title would not be 'sir Rex,' unless we were at some kind of Renaissance Festival. You would just call me 'sir.'

Sydex stepped into the center of where the couples had gathered, held up his hands and said, "Okay, we're getting ready to start, so if I could just get everybody to gather over here so we can go over a few safety rules, that would be great."

Rex and Lucy joined the circle as the instructor ran through Rope Bondage Safety 101. He then grabbed a section of his own rope and said, "Okay, let's start with a basic wrist cuff on your bottoms, right arm behind her back, loose ends facing out toward you. We'll work our way into some simple ties and then get onto the harder stuff as we progress. You can use a lark's head to start if you like to keep it simple, as long as you're looping back to create some reverse tension. I need to see two fingers clearance in any areas of major blood flow. So let's have fun and be safe."

Rex moved Lucy into the correct position and worked on making a clean-looking wrist cuff. The next move involved looping around Lucy's torso and as he started to draw the rope around her she said, "Wait a second, is that going to snag my sweater?"

"What? No. I don't think so. Are you calling what you're wearing a sweater?"

"Yes, of course, it's a sweater, look at the fabric. See the weave?"

"If you're calling this a sweater, it's the tightest sweater I've ever seen."

"Are you guys okay?" Somehow Sydex had appeared right next to them without Rex hearing a sound.

"What?" Rex said, "Oh, yeah. We're fine. She's just worried about the rope snagging her sweater."

"Hmmm, this is pretty decent cotton rope. No nylon, right? It probably won't snag."

"Probably?" Lucy said. "Screw it." And with that, she reached for the bottom hem of her sweater and pulled it over her head in one smooth motion to reveal a black sports bra. She then worked the sweater over the cuff and the length of rope hanging from her wrist and grinned at Sydex.

"Now it definitely won't snag," Sydex said, "but I should tell you we're doing an upper torso harness that's designed to, um, lift and separate, so he's going to be running lengths, um, in between and around."

"So, lose the bra, too, I'm guessing," Lucy said.

"The tie will definitely work better that way."

"Right." Lucy discreetly turned her back to Rex and Sydex and with another deftly executed overhead motion became topless, saying, "Keep tying, sir."

Rex laid a hand on her bare shoulder and slowly began to loop the rope around her, feeling a mix of anxiety and excitement. Had things already gone too far? How was this going to end up? But as he focused on the twists and turns used to change direction and enhance her form, he lost himself in the procedure, working to keep the knots straight and as elegant as possible. He moved in front of her and looked down, not feeling lecherous so much as curious and joyful. Her breasts were indeed a sight to behold with perfectly shaped pink nipples that had stiffened in the cool air. She was beautiful and compliant, occasionally making little noises of what sounded like pleasure as he cinched her into positions that helplessly exposed her.

"Are you okay?" has asked her softly.

"Yes, I'm fine. Are you enjoying yourself?"

"I have to admit, I am. What's François doing?"

"Turn me around, so I can watch."

Rex guided her around so she could watch the other couples and noticed that she was the only one still wearing slacks, which caused him to deeply inhale, imagining what would happen if they moved to the lower torso.

"Ideally I need to get over there and try to become his new best friend. I need a last name or something to stay out of jail."

"Shhh, he's looking at me. I think he likes my knockers."

"I can't believe you just said 'knockers.'"

"Yeah, well, I know he wants to be my friend even if he's on the fence about you. Maybe he should tie me up and you can switch to the little gymnast chick."

"I don't think that's a good idea, Luce. The guy probably killed Amy."

"Why, Rex, I do believe you're jealous. That's very sweet, but I can take care of myself."

Rex pulled a loop tight, which caused Lucy to say, "Oh!"

"I'm well aware of that, Luce—just let me handle it, okay?"

"Yes, sir. You're in charge here."

They completed the tie and then moved on to three variations. Sydex walked amongst the couples, looking at the bends, twists, and positions of the limbs relative to various classic submissive poses. He offered advice, critiques, and encouragement as he walked through, tugging at a loose end here and suggesting a different way to tie off the bights there. Rex again flashed back on summer camp where he learned some of the basic knots that were currently holding Lucy's bonds in place.

"All right, let's free up our models for a moment, let them catch their breath, rediscover some blood flow and take a few minutes break. Everybody having fun? Everybody getting some nice rope marks?" said Sydex.

There were sounds of affirmation as Rex began unspooling Lucy. "Perfect. Here's my chance to get acquainted."

Lucy gracefully pulled her top back on, neglecting the bra, and said, "Go get him, tiger; I have to visit the loo. I think you've squeezed all the excess moisture out of my upper extremities."

Rex recoiled his ropes and watched François from the corner of his eye. He grabbed what was left of his drink and gradually drifted toward him while pretending to stop and look at the gear, clothing, and rope that were now cluttering the play area. As he got close enough to start a conversation, he noticed that François was using what appeared to be hemp.

"Hey, do you like using the hemp? I got some dyed cotton stuff for this class, but I was looking at this, too. This is nice," Rex said, as he pointed at a coil on the floor.

"Yes, cotton slips too easy. Hemp has a better bite but cotton is a good starter rope."

"Yeah, that's what I've heard and I am a newbie. Have you been doing this for a while?"

"A while."

"Yeah, okay. Hey, my name is Rex, by the way—Rex Armstrong." He stuck his hand out.

François accepted the handshake saying. "That's a great scene name—Rex. Like a super-hero, no?"

Rex laughed. "Yeah, I guess, except it's my real name whether I'm in the scene or in real life. And you are 'François,' right?

"Yes. François."

"Is that what you go by in real life, too? I mean, I use my real name just because it's simpler, plus I don't really care who knows."

"Lucky you. Some of us have to be more discreet. Will you excuse me? I need to get a refill."

"Sure, I'll go with you. I didn't think the bar would be open. Usually, on bondage nights there's no drinking," Rex said, trailing François down the hall.

"It's quite silly, these rules. In Europe, things are much more relaxed and everyone is more tastefully dressed. More of a grown-up affair than here."

Rex inhaled the other dude's scent, a pleasant, subtle aroma as he noted François' relaxed stride back toward the bar. In some ways he envied this European attitude to the scene, which attempted to lift the deviant behavior and elevate it to a different set of mores that belonged to the upper class. The conversation was making him feel better about himself, while at the same causing a longing for more classy surroundings and participants.

"Yeah, I've heard the clubs over there are much more posh and attract a higher class of kinkster. I'd love to get an invite to one of those affairs."

"Yes, it's because they are expensive and selective about who knows what and who is afforded membership. Tell me, Rex. This girl you are with. Is she yours exclusively?"

"No, she's a neighbor and a friend of mine. She's not really in the scene. She's kind of doing this as a favor."

"So, you are not a couple, then."

Rex swallowed. "No, we're both quite single."

The two men ordered refills and as they waited, François turned to Rex and said, "Are you serious about that notion, Rex? The desire to see how the other half enjoys these kinds of activities? A peek behind the curtain? Because it does happen here, but not in places like this. Private parties, usually in spacious homes of the very rich, very beautiful and very perverted. What would you do to get inside those doors, my friend?"

Rex laughed a bit too loud. "Gee, I don't know, buddy. What do you want, a kidney?"

"Nothing that permanent. Allow me to use your model for the second half of the class. You take mine and at the end of the session, I will give you a key to the kingdom."

"Um," Rex said, just as Lucy joined them at the bar.

"What's up, boys?" she asked.

"Um, my new pal here just propositioned me," Rex said.

"Really?" Lucy said. "I didn't realize that was in your repertoire, Rex."

"It's not."

"Oh, she is a pure delight," said François, "but not completely accurate, my dear. Mr. Super Hero wants some information from me, and I want to do a more intricate tie on you and suspend you from the ceiling like the goddess that you are. I offered him a fair trade."

"And what did he say?" asked Lucy.

They both looked at Rex. He couldn't read what Lucy was thinking, but she had a challenging look on her face. François, on the other hand, was smiling like a warm reptile.

"Fine," said Rex. "What's your sub's name?"

"You may call her whatever you like. Come along, goddess. Have you ever been suspended by your delicate limbs before?"

"Why, no, I don't think so," Lucy said as they walked away from Rex, arm in arm.

"Fuck," Rex said out loud to no one.

Lucy looked at him over her shoulder and winked as they disappeared into the darkness. Rex felt a wave of nausea wash over him. Lucy was obviously flirting with François, but Rex couldn't divine her true intentions. Was she really attracted to him? Was she doing it to play him for the information Rex needed to get out of Dutch with the cops? Was she doing it to make Rex jealous? He reconsidered the whole idea of dragging her into this as a bad idea. He dropped money on the bar to pay for his drink, took a big pull off it and let the icy whiskey flow down his throat.

He walked back to the semi-circle of mostly naked bodies and breathed a sigh of relief when he saw that Lucy still had her clothes on. She was deep in some kind of conversation with François and he was watching her, intently listening to whatever was coming out her mouth. François appeared to be hypnotized and Rex could only hope that Lucy was extracting as much information as he was providing.

When he got back to where he'd left his supplies, François's still-naked model now stood where Lucy used to be, her hands clasped behind her back, chin pointed up, nipples erect.

"Apparently there's been a change in the lineup and you're stuck with me, young lady. My name is Rex. Who might you be?"

The naked girl stuck out a hand and said, "You can call me Sheena, sir, and I look forward to playing with you. Does my nudity offend you?"

Rex laughed and said, "Not at all, why?"

"Well, I noticed your other partner was clothed…but now I see she's getting back into the swing of things."

"Yes, well. What?"

Rex glanced over to see that Lucy had already removed her top and was now sliding her slacks down her long, toned legs. Rex cleared his throat and brushed some sweat off his forehead.

"Okay," Sydex said. He raised his hands to call attention to his latest pronouncement. "We're going to go ahead and get started on the second half, where we're going to work on some ties that encompass the lower limbs. We're also going to bring the chains down from the rafters and do a little suspension work, if any of you want to hang out, heh, heh, heh… Let's start with an ankle cuff, on the left ankle and then we're going to wrap around the calf like we did earlier on the arm tie."

Rex refocused his attention back to the ropes as he worked his way around Sheena's compact and very wiry body. "You're in great shape. François told me you're a gymnast?"

"A long time ago in high school. No, I'm just a bean counter at Metro, I'm afraid. Not a gymnast."

"Oh, really? Metro, huh? I think one of François's other friends worked at Metro. Do you know Amy?"

"I don't think so. Is that her real name?"

"I don't know. Who can keep track? I just heard she worked for Metro, too, so I thought you might know her."

"No, sorry. It's a big outfit and I just started so I hardly know anybody."

"Okay. How did you meet François?"

"Met him at this party in Potomac. It's mostly a swingers' scene but there's a little BDSM going on, too. I went with my girlfriend. She's not really into any of this stuff—just goes because there's supposedly a lot of rich people there, like rich military dudes and stuff. So we went for that, but then I met François and he asked me if I'd ever been like tied up and stuff and I said, 'No, but I'd try anything once,' and then he was like, 'Well, just step right over here,' and I was like, 'Okay, I'll do that,' and then the next thing I know, there I was, naked as a jaybird getting all tied up and stuff.'"

Rex now knew why François wanted to switch—one possible reason, anyway. Sheena talked non-stop, to the point where Rex found himself looking through the toy bag for a ball gag even though he was sure he hadn't brought one. With this kind of intense tying, the bottom had to be able to communicate if she was feeling distressed, but Rex was the one struggling with the situation.

Although he was trying to pay attention to the ropes, knots, and instructor, he was most concerned with what was happening between François and Lucy. He didn't want to stare, but she was now completely naked and seemed to be, if not enjoying herself, at least comfortable. How did he miss this part of her personality? After all that hesitation on his part she seemed to be quite the willing subject.

He craned his neck, trying to get a better look, and felt guilty about it. He was getting what he always wanted but the feelings of jealousy were hard to ignore. He wanted to be the one running the ropes around her. He hadn't counted on the emotional cost of sharing the experience with the rest of the class and especially François. He brushed a sheen of perspiration off his forehead as he heard Sydex announce they would be bringing the ceiling lines down.

Whatever Sheena was talking about was now flowing into his head and spilling out the other side, leaving no impression whatsoever. He finished the tie in a disconnected haze as he glanced over and saw some of the other participants gathered around Lucy and François, watching as loops were attached to combinations of D-rings and O-rings. Soon enough, Lucy had slipped the bonds of planet earth and was hoisted into the sky, a living sculpture for all to see and admire.

Even Sheena stopped talking long enough to witness the grand ascension and there was a smattering of applause. Rex looked away, feeling queasy and unsettled. He pretended to be adjusting the rope around Sheena's thigh—a worrisome and key area for blood flow problems—but his mind was flipping through a horrible set of outcomes to this little debacle.

Lucy and François, together forever, an unlikely match that now fell into the category of bonds that no man can cast asunder. The two of them laughing about Rex's predicament. There would be no revelation of secret info. He would learn nothing. The cops would come back, Rex would take a poke at one of them and be tossed into jail as they promised. He knew from the cop shows that they could hold him for 24 hours without filing charges, but chances were they would file charges because the fingerprint on the cock ring would match his thumb.

He'd be fighting accusations that he killed Amy, a girl he didn't even really know. A girl whose last name was hidden. A girl he played with at a sex club—a fact that would come out in the trial. They had DNA evidence on him. Once the people at work found out, he would be ruined. He'd have a reputation as a perverted sex killer, the IRS would swoop in to take whatever was left, and Rex's life would be over.

Wellborn, whoever he actually was, would disavow all knowledge and who was going to believe his story about being recruited by an unnamed spy agency? Generals selling drone technology? What the hell was he thinking? He was fucking doomed. He dropped his hands and walked in a trance toward Lucy, who was now twirling slowly in the air, six feet off the floor.

Everybody was standing around, admiring the work, and Rex tried to blend in by checking out the ties, admiring the pose, nodding in admiration to François.

"All right, gang, let's bring her down. Everybody check in with your partners and start wrapping things up. The club needs to get ready for the next event; I think it's leather night or something. But let's give ourselves a little round of applause."

And so they all did their version of a golf clap. Rex watched carefully as his neighbor was lowered safely to the ground. He returned to Sheena, thanked her for being cooperative and began untying her while she continued to talk. He finished releasing her and decided a drink might be in order. He would go to the bar, have a stabilizer, then come back and talk to Lucy and François as if nothing had happened.

He followed his own plan and floated toward the booze. He heard himself place an order, took a healthy slug, and wavered back toward the main play area. He emerged into the space, ready to confront his tormentors and immediately noticed that François and his tools were gone. Lucy appeared in front of him, fully dressed, hair tousled and said, "Well, that was weird. Did you get me a drink or just one for yourself?"

Rex took a sip and handed it to her. "Help yourself, babe."

Lucy took a big swig. Rex watched her, looking to see if anything in her appearance indicated a change in her personality. Had anything changed? Was there something different about her?

"Are you okay? Anything sore or hurting?"

She lowered the glass long enough to say, "No, I'm fine. Let's get the flock out of here," and then handed it back to him.

"Hold on a sec and let me finish this, will you? I need to decompress." Rex guided her to a rickety round table with two stackable, steel-framed chairs—temporary furniture for temporary friends.

Rex stared at the tabletop, afraid to ask more questions. "Did you find out anything? Do we have a last name?"

"Last name? Is this your drink or mine?"

"Take the drink, Luce. François? Did we learn anything about him? That's why we're here, remember? You spent some quality time with him? What were you guys talking about?"

"Oh, god. He has a thing for blonde American chicks, obviously. And rope. Typical Eurotrash big mouth. He grew up in Switzerland, daddy's a banker with the IMF, he's living off a trust fund, drives a BMW, hangs out at bottle clubs, blah-blah-blah."

Rex felt a wave of recognition and relief settle onto the table with them. "He sounds like, dare I say it, a bit of a douchebag."

Lucy took another drink and said, "Total fucking douchebag. He wants to take me to St. Martin, or Biarritz, or somewhere like that. Totally full of shit."

"I see and was he, um, did he act like a gentleman with you, while you were working together?"

"Well, as much as a man can be while he's tying ropes around your coochie. You know, Rex, I sort of understand why you like this stuff. It's kind of like a huge tease. You're so close to the goods and yet, you're not supposed to touch. Kind of weird. I mean, wouldn't you rather tie a girl up at home and then, you know, do whatever you want without everybody gawking? It was kind of fun getting pulled up into the air and twirling around but it was starting to hurt my knee a little."

Rex listened to her rant, feeling a bit better about things, feeling the dark clouds over his head lightening in color, perhaps to a gray flannel. He took the drink back and had a sip, feeling the familiar and satisfying burn of the alcohol in his mouth.

"Sorry about that, Luce, I didn't know the class was going to include suspension. I don't suppose in all this fun he happened to mention his last name to you or how you might get in touch with him? Did he ask for your number?"

"Only about ten times, but this isn't my first rodeo, Rexy. I know what the name of the game is. Here." She offered Rex an elegant, ivory-shaded business card with raised handwriting that read,

"Francois Bellamy, 202.309.6996."

Rex took the card between his fingers and saw his own salvation.

A sliver of hope rendered onto a tiny slip of fortified paper.

"Oh, he also told me to give this to you as part of the bargain." She handed over a rendition of a miniature skeleton key made of solid brass with a coiled whip logo stamped into the top of the key. "I did, good, right Rex?"

"Yes, Lucy, you did very good."

"So now we turn this over to the cops and get you out of trouble, right?"

"Not just yet. Come on, let's get out of this shithole."

CHAPTER 13

Rex stuffed the ropes and other gear into his saddlebags, made sure Lucy was situated on the back end of the bike and roared off toward home, his mind racing with possibilities. He'd already decided he would use François's contact info to see what he could learn on his own before turning the case over to the DC cops. He put the bike to sleep in the garage, kissed Lucy on the cheek, said goodbye and took his treasures up to his home office. He Googled the name and the phone number on the card then examined the key in more detail. It was classy work, which caused him to Google "custom-made skeleton keys." This dunked him into the eccentric world of steampunk.

He went to all the major fetish sites, looking for a similar key with a coiled whip logo, but found nothing. After his quick tour through the wonderland of digital research, Rex didn't know much more than when he started. François Bellamy was probably the dude's real name and phone number. He was into rope bondage and domination, but mostly rope. This might be enough to keep the cops from throwing Rex in jail, but he wished had a little more to turn over.

Technically, François hadn't given Rex the card, so it might be considered poor form for Rex to reach out to him directly. This took him back to the question of the key. The key to what? And what did all this have to do with the generals and drone technology and why the hell would Wellborn care about any of this? As he sat there thinking about smoking and having a drink to go with it, the computer bonged. It was an email notification letting him know he'd received a message on one of the fetish sites from somebody called "Master of Keys." He navigated to the site and opened a very classy looking invite to a "Night of Delectable and Masked Debauchery." By RSVP'ing to the invite, his application would be reviewed and directions to the party site would be provided upon acceptance. The party was the following Saturday night.

"Hmmm," Rex said to himself. "Who are these freaks?"

He texted Chester and offered to buy him a drink, a ploy that never failed to get his attention. Then he texted Wellborn and told him he had additional information on François. He rifled through business cards, restaurant receipts, and assorted scraps of paper on his desktop looking for the contact information from the cops. What were their names again? Couldn't remember. Chester responded first—big surprise.

"I'd love a drink, mate. Booked this evening with "Swingers Night" at the club, but pop by tomorrow after 2. I'll need one by then."

Wellborn was maintaining radio silence, so Rex settled into a quiet evening at home, watching Twilight Zone reruns until he fell asleep on the couch. Waking a little later, he checked his phone for messages, saw nothing, and texted Lucy a big-time thank-you. She wasn't responding, either, and he let his mind wonder where she was, what she was doing and who she was doing it with. The sting of jealousy shot through him like a jagged arrow as he relived the vision of her and François.

He tried to remember the last time he'd had such a reaction—a stab wound of emotion carved into his psyche and attached to a person in his life whom he was connected with, if only in a most cursory way. Why did it bother him so much? He finally went to bed, but flipped and flopped for awhile until he fell asleep.

He awoke the next morning to the sounds of somebody knocking on his door, a sound that he was not used to hearing. He pulled himself to the front door, peered out through the peephole and saw two dudes dressed like squares.

"Fuck. Hang on a second, fellas," he shouted at the door. He threw on a pair of jeans, forgoing the underwear, and found a black t-shirt on the floor, which he pulled on before pulling the door open. "DC's finest, I presume?"

Span and Franklin walked through the door with heads pivoting, already looking for clues.

"You alone in here, Mr. Armstrong?" Span asked.

"Yes, of course," Rex said. "Let me ask you something—why are cops always asking that question? What's the difference who I'm with?"

"The difference, Mr. Wisenheimer, is that if you were not alone and if there were another person in here hiding behind a door with a weapon, we would kind of like to know about that," Franklin said. His eyes scanned the corners of the room. Apparently, he was operating on some kind of cop autopilot setting.

"Okay, well, there is no other person hiding behind the door, or elsewhere," Rex said.

"That's super, Mr. Armstrong. Lovely night at the pervo club and you came home alone?" said Franklin.

"Something like that," Rex said. "Why are you here, invading my space at 9 am on Sunday morning? I thought we were going to reconnect early next week."

"Technically, it is early next week," said Span. "Have you uncovered any new information you might like to share?"

Rex began the morning ritual of coffee making and said, "Yes, I have. Do you guys want some coffee? I'm having some. Sorry I don't have any donuts to go with it." Rex looked at their faces, devoid of any emotion. "Just a joke, fellas." He hit the power button on the coffee machine, went to his desk, found François's card and handed it to Span. "This is the guy I was telling you about. I'm pretty sure that's his real last name."

Span handed the card to Franklin, who looked down his nose at it and said, "And he gave this to you why?"

"Actually he didn't give it to me, he gave it to a friend of mine. The girl you met the other night. He also gave me this." Rex held up the key and tossed it underhand toward Franklin, who caught it without trying very hard.

Franklin inspected the key. "More kinky shit. Who the fuck are these people?"

"They also invited me to a party at an undisclosed location next week," Rex said.

"Well, how lovely for you. A party, you say? Too bad you won't be able to go since you'll be, like, in jail, huh?" Span said. "What do you think, Detective Franklin, shall we track down Mr. Bellamy, bring him in for questioning along with Mr. Armstrong here and see which one rats first?"

"Let's not do that, guys, Rex said. "Listen. I'm meeting with another associate this afternoon, a source that may know more about these people and these parties and what happened to Amy. Can you give me another week before we start arresting people?"

Span took the business card back from Franklin and pulled out a cellphone as turned away from Rex and began punching in a number.

"The world would run better if you were in charge, wouldn't it, Rex?" said Franklin.

"I'm just saying, assuming you can even find François using a phone number, what are you going to ask him? I mean, wouldn't you like to have some more details before you barge in and start asking questions?" The aroma of fresh-brewed coffee began to fill the apartment as Rex nervously watched Span, the guy he considered to be the good cop, now talking into his phone and reading the number on the card. From what Rex could figure out, Span wasn't actually calling Francois but was, in fact, asking somebody on the other end where the phone was currently located.

"How about you let us do the police work and you do the kinky shit? That way everybody does what they do best. And actually, our best work is all about barging in and asking questions, as evidenced by our current situation here." Franklin finished his speech to Rex, and then turned his attention back to Span. "What do you got, Billy?"

"Union Station. He may be taking a powder. Let's blow."

Franklin tossed the key back to Rex. "Do not fucking leave town, Rex, we got your number, too. We'll be back in touch." They exited in quick fashion with a slam of the door.

"Shit," Rex said. He and pulled a coffee cup out of the cabinet. He tried to relax by reading the Sunday paper but he couldn't sit still, now dreading the chaos he had started. If François was able to board a train before the cops got to him, the cops were sure to come back looking for him. He puttered around the apartment for a while and happily left for his meeting with Chester right after lunch. His mind raced around from one unpleasant thought to the next as the miles ticked by on his way to the club.

He pulled into an empty parking lot, turned off the motorcycle and hit the door buzzer, tapping his foot waiting for entry. The door opened and Chester's head popped out, his eyes blinking in the sunlight.

"Reximus Maximus, himself," Chester said. "Do come in. I just finished and realized I've got a liter of Scotch with our name on it. Assuming it's not too early for whiskey."

"It's never too early for me, old bean. We can put it in coffee if need be." Rex stepped through the door, watched Chester throw the lock and then followed him back toward the office.

"How are the swingers?" Rex took a seat across from Chester's desk.

"Truly sexually obsessed people, my friend. But they aren't afraid to spend money or fornicate in the most unexpected places." Chester produced two glasses, checked them for cleanliness, and began to pour. "Need ice?"

"No, I'll pretend I'm British in honor of your presence."

"There's a good lad. Bottoms up."

They clinked glasses as Rex took a tiny sip of the room-temperature hooch and watched Chester take a healthy swig.

"Whoa, you are a manly dude. Unexpected places meaning what, the bathrooms?"

"I wish. The bathrooms are a given. On top of the bar, under tables, in the parking lot, up against walls. I caught two of them trying to get into the stockroom, totally nude of course attempting to jimmy the lock. Can you imagine? A stockroom full of boxes without any real usable surface area?"

"Crazy business you're in, isn't it?"

"Quite bizarre. So why are you darkening my door, Rex? If this is about that fucked-up situation with Amy, I don't want to hear anything about it. I like to keep my interactions with the police as limited as possible, even though quite of few of them are way kinked up."

"Oh, I'm sure," Rex said. He reached into his pocket for the key. "The uniforms, the leather, the restraint devices, the whole power exchange thing." He found the key, pulled it out and placed it on Chester's desk next to his glass, which still had a finger of scotch in it.

Chester looked at the key, obviously recognized it, but made no move to pick it up. "Where did you get this?"

"If I told you, you would be forced against your will to learn more about the Amy incident and you just told me you don't want to know any more, so why don't you tell me what you know about the key?"

Chester looked at it again and this time picked it up like it might be hot. "Well, Rexy, what you have here is an invite into the upper reaches of kink heaven. It's called, 'Fouet Enroule.' I think it's French for 'coiled whip,' which makes sense because as you can see, it's got this little picture of a coiled whip on it." Chester slid the key back to Rex and sat there like a silent Buddha.

"And…?" Rex said.

Chester pursed his lips and said nothing.

"What the fuck? You are like the biggest blabbermouth in the scene and you're not going to tell me anything about this? Do they have dirty pictures with you and a goat or something, Chester? What gives?"

Chester poured more Scotch into his glass and then topped off Rex's even though he'd barely touched it.

"Okay, here's the deal, mate. I'll tell you what I know but this conversation is not happening, understood?"

"Sure, fine, whatever. What are they going to do, take away your birthday?"

"Well, first of all, most people in the scene don't know that they even exist. It's the stuff of myths. But here's what I can divulge." Chester hunched his shoulders and leaned in close as if somebody might be listening in and for a brief second, Rex saw Wellborn's face floating in front of his eyes. Would the Feds bug the office of a guy running a fetish club? Wellborn had known the name of Chester's club.

"I've always heard that they are mostly European and American fat cats. Captains of industry, political leaders, maybe a few celebrities—rich fucks. Right? They're so paranoid about having their identities discovered, nobody really knows who the other members are. Their gatherings usually require full masks and costumes, very "Eyes Wide Shut" kind of stuff."

"Seriously? This is real life?"

"Oh, it gets better. So the parties are usually a smattering of the regular kinks, there will be a dungeon room, some bondage, orgy rooms, blah blah blah, but they're really known for the edgy stuff. Single tail whips, fire, asphyxiation, people routinely get hurt at these things and sometimes they don't like it as much as they think they might."

"So that's it? A bunch of rich freaks in costumes nearly killing each other? It sounds like an excellent idea to me."

"Ahhh, but they have a mean streak, Rex." Chester took a big swig from his glass and looked at Rex. "You're not drinking—are you trying to make me feel bad?" Rex took another sip and let the liquid slide down as easily as possible. He really wasn't a Scotch fan, and it was still fairly early in the day.

"What do you mean, 'mean streak?'"

"Did you ever hear about Carnival Bill?"

"No. Who was Carnival Bill?"

"Right, yeah, so Carnival Bill was in the CIA, pretty high up, I think, and kinky as hell. He was into the whole "baby girl" thing, pigtails and knee socks or whatever."

"Yeah, that shit is kind of weird."

"Not my cup of poison, either. Anyway, Carnival Bill is into the 'Littles,' and he's a charter member of Fouet Enroule and he's a spy, so you would think that he would know better. But he helped start the group or something like that. Anyway, he does something to piss them off, nobody can even remember what it was but some people say he handed one of those keys, a key just like that, to somebody that the group didn't want coming to the party. Know what I mean?

The group finds out about it, so what do they do? They out him to the press, his family, they tell everybody who knows Carnival Bill that he gets his kicks out of hanging out with women dressed up and acting like little girls. His career is ruined, it's on the front page of *The Washington Post*. He wasn't married at the time, but the bastards tracked down his parents, people from work, neighbors, anybody they could to shame him out of existence."

"Wow. So what happened to him?"

"Blew his fucking brains out in his basement."

"You're shitting me."

"Look it up. It was all over the papers back then."

"Wow."

"Right. Wow. So actually, I don't want to know who gave you the key or what you intend to do with it. More Scotch?"

"No, I'm fine. But that was in the old days. You're very out about yourself and what you do. Nobody cares about that shit anymore. What are you afraid of?"

"It wasn't that long ago, and there are still plenty of boogeymen out there, Rex. One loud-mouthed Baptist preacher can kill this business. Or how about an intrusive enema from the IRS? They could cancel my liquor license, not extend my business license, talk to the insurance people, there are all kinds of things motivated individuals could do if they wanted to get to me, so I really want nothing to with the cats from the Coiled Whip."

"So in other words, if I had an extra invitation to the masked ball, you wouldn't go with me, is that right?"

Chester took another swig and looked at Rex, his eye hovering above the edge of the tumbler.

"Are you saying you have an extra ticket, Rex? I might be already going anyway; you wouldn't know because I would be in costume and would not admit to you, even now, that I knew anything about it."

"So what does that mean, you wouldn't go with me?"

"Wouldn't you prefer to take a girl? Were you instructed to

bring a woman? They are usually quite specific about what is permitted and what is not. Do not fuck with these people, Rex. You work for the government, don't you?"

"Last I heard," Rex said. He drained his glass of the harsh, smoky liquid.

Rex said goodbye to Chester and felt his phone vibrate on the ride home. He went into the apartment and found a text from Wellborn.

"Greetings Mr. Armstrong, can we meet and debrief tomorrow at lunch? Same place, 1:00?"

Rex texted back that would be fine and began flipping through TV channels looking for something to hold his interest. He settled on a black-and-white western with Gary Cooper for background noise and then decided to check his email, which revealed a coy message from someone named "Sheena." Who the hell was… "Oh, shit," Rex said to himself, "the rope bunny chatterbox from the workshop."

He chuckled to himself as he read a very polite thank you note from Sheena, who also suggested they might get together for coffee or happy hour sometime. She provided a phone number in case he was so inclined. Rex put her contact info into his phone punched in a text message to her, identifying himself and offering to take her up on her offer.

He settled back into Gary Cooper when the phone vibrated again. Assuming it was Wellborn confirming, Rex was a bit surprised when the quick response came from Sheena saying she was out with her "vanilla friends" near Dupont Circle and was "bored out of her mind." Rex weighed further contact with her, balancing her tendency to talk non-stop against her tight, gymnast-like body and that fact that she somehow might be mixed up with Amy's disappearance. Didn't she say something about swingers parties at rich people's houses? Was she in with the Coiled Whip crowd?

Rex bit his lip and asked if she'd like to be rescued by joining him for a drink at the place across the street. Assuming she would say "no" based on the short notice, he almost dropped the phone when she answered back in the affirmative and an "SYS ☺" for See You Soon," complete with the smiley face.

"What the fuck? Really?" It all seemed fishy, too easy and too convenient to be true but Rex found a clean shirt, ran his fingers through his hair, checked his cash situation and got ready to walk across the street. It was Sunday night, a traditional day of drink and celebration for the District, even with the workweek looming in the near future. The bar might be crowded, so Rex decided to go early in case he needed to work his way into two seats.

Rex walked over, lucked into a seat at the bar and ordered his regular from Joe.

"What are you doing here on a Sunday, my good man? Don't you ever get a day off?"

Joe slid a beer in front of him and said, "I'm off Mondays and Tuesdays like most barkeeps, as you've probably noticed. Kind of early for you, isn't it?"

"Well, supposedly a young lady is joining me for an afternoon cocktail."

"Excellent. Would that be Ms. Lucy?"

Rex winced thinking about making a date with someone he wasn't sure he was even interested in when he would in fact, rather be spending time with Lucy. "Unfortunately, no, this is somebody I met at an event the other night who just called me out of the blue."

"She called you? Nice. Tell me, Rex, what is your secret with the ladies?"

"Well, I have all my teeth, most of my hair, a motorcycle, and a job. As we get older, the odds tilt to our favor, young man. You'll find out someday."

Joe laughed and clinked his coffee cup to Rex's beer. "So it has nothing to do with your magnetic personality?"

Rex smiled. "Well, that doesn't hurt, either." He knew Joe was bullshitting him but didn't mind.

"So what are you up to with the new chick? Have you given up on Lucy? I see you guys in here all the time drinking together, what's the story there?"

"I think we're destined to just remain friends. We don't have enough in common."

"Really? I'm not so sure, dude. Seems to be some kind of connection there. Have you ever tried to, you know, take her out on a real date?"

"What is that? A real date? I'm not even sure I know what that means."

"Dating as in part of the courtship ritual, Rex. As in a date that will lead somewhere besides the bedroom. I think that's what she's looking for, but what do I know?"

Rex furrowed his brow, considering these pearls of wisdom. "You know what, you may be onto something here. Maybe there are some possibilities that I haven't completely explored. That is helpful advice."

"Just doing my job, bub."

Rex continued working on his beer while taking note of the various barflies around him and whether any of them were about to leave so Rex could grab another stool for Sheena. Joe's words were still echoing through his skull as Sheena appeared, wearing tight black jeans and a flouncy top that showed a bit of shallow cleavage.

"Hello, sir," she said with a smile and threw a quick hug on him. "Thanks for the rescue. They were all talking about marriage plans, kids, guys they're dating that they don't really like, cats, and

Facebook. I was ready to run into traffic. This is a cool place, I've never been here before, Kind of a sports bar or something, right? I mean, I don't really watch sports, but I don't care if other people do. I hope you don't think I was being too pushy, sending you a message, it's just hard to find people with similar interests sometimes, and I kind of liked hanging out with you. But I don't want to interfere if you're like seeing that girl you were with at the thing. Oh, hi. Can I have a chardonnay or something?" she said to Joe.

Rex motioned to Joe to put the wine on his tab as he turned away toward the coolers.

Joe poured a glass of wine for Sheena and discreetly floated out of earshot as Rex offered her his seat. "So what did you think of the workshop?" he asked. "Did you enjoy it?"

"Oh, sure, it was fine. I really did it as a favor to François. I wouldn't have gone to something like that on my own."

"So what are you saying, you're not really part of the whole kink scene?"

"Oh, it's not that, I'm as kinky as all get out. I like the exhibition part and the rope and the submission, but I'm just saying I wouldn't usually attend a workshop. I prefer to practice more in private. Know what I mean?"

Rex chuckled and felt his body heat going up. "I do know what you mean. Are you and François close?"

She took a sip of wine and shook her head. "I don't think François is close to anybody. He's just a guy who's charming and seems to have plenty of money but no real job. I think he's just rich for a living."

"That's the job I want."

"You and me both. So, what's your deal, Rex? You seem to know your way around. What do you do in real life?"

"Work for the Feds doing media stuff, I have an ex-wife causing me grief with the IRS and I'm trying to solve a mystery that maybe you can help me with. François used to hang out with a chick named Amy and I think I saw him at a party the other night that was happening at a French defense contractors building across the street from my apartment. Do you know anything about any of that?"

She took another sip of wine and said, "I've never met an Amy and I don't know anything about the French company but I do think he's French." Rex felt in his pocket for the skeleton key, pulled it out and laid it on the bar next to Sheena's wine glass. "Ever see one of these?"

Sheena seemed to freeze for a second and clearly recognized the key. "Oh, you got a key. You do know your way around, Rex."

"You've seen one of these before?"

"Sure, François has one just like it. You need one of those to get into the…"

"The what?"

"So, you've never been?"

"Been where?"

"To one of those parties where you need one of those keys to get into."

"No. What kinds of parties are they?"

"Rough, Rex. They play hard."

"So you have been to one. Is it the swingers party thing out in Potomac you were telling me about?"

She shook her head, stared down at the bar and said, "Truth is, I'm not sure where the party was. Somewhere out in the burbs. Everybody wears masks; it's kind of creepy."

"But you went to one with François, and what happened to you?"

"Nothing happened to me, we just kind of walked through and hung out for awhile but the mood was really dark. I didn't like it. Lots of heavy S and M stuff, you know, whips and chains, people screaming, all kinds of dungeon gear. It was a little too heavy for me."

"You went with François and he was wearing a mask, too?"

"Yeah, everybody wears a mask. He disappeared on me for awhile, came back kind of breathing hard and said we should leave."

"Wow."

"Yeah, so what about you and that blonde you brought to the rope thingy, is she your girlfriend?"

"No, we're just friends."

"And you're not married?"

"Not anymore, no."

"And you're not really seeing anybody, like as a steady thing."

"Nope, I'm afraid not."

"And that's because you're like recovering from your last bad relationship or something?"

Rex took a big swig of beer. "Yeah, I guess you could say that."

"And you live close by, by yourself?"

"All by myself, right across the street."

"Is it a nice place? Seems like kind of an upscale neighborhood."

"Yeah, it's nice. Kind of expensive, but it's comfortable. Maybe even a bit too comfortable. I may never leave despite the damage to my bank account. Where are you at?"

"Columbia Heights. It's okay."

"And you and François, you're not romantically involved?"

"Oh, no. He's not really my type. Kind of fidgety and secretive."

"I see. And what is your type? You have a type?"

"Mmmm, I don't know. You're kind of an interesting guy, Rex. Maybe somebody like you. You seem pretty nice."

"And not too fidgety?"

She smiled and bumped against his shoulder, smiling as a bit of wine leaked out of the corner of her mouth.

"Not too fidgety at all."

"I see. Would you like to see where I live to see if I become more fidgety in a more intimate setting?"

"Why, Rex. I do believe you're propositioning me. What kind of a girl do you think I am?"

Rex smiled back at her and said, "Oh, just the kind of girl who enjoys walking around naked and being tied up. Somebody who could be my type."

"I need to use the restroom. Hold that thought. Is it in the back?"

Rex nodded and watched her head toward the ladies room.

"What the hell am I doing?" he asked himself as he pictured the last time he left this bar with a woman. It was Lucy that time and he ended up rousted by the cops and puking into the bushes. He didn't feel like puking now, in fact, he felt perfectly fine and capable of taking Sheena for a ride on the temporary love train.

"You doing all right, buddy? Want a refill?"

Joe reappeared as Rex squinted into a beer glass that was mostly empty. "Give me a minute. We may be moving the party across the street."

"Living the dream, aren't you?"

"I reckon."

Sheena returned, repositioned herself into the chair and said, "Now, as you were saying?" She was sitting close to him and he could feel her presence pushing against him, their legs touching under the bar.

"I was saying I have plenty of refreshment over at my place; it's quieter and the prices are more affordable."

"I see. Got rope?"

"A whole bag full."

He felt her hand on his thigh as she said, "I remember that part. I'm ready whenever you are, sir."

Rex closed the tab, guided Sheena off the stool, turned toward the door and walked right into Lucy.

"Well, well, well, and who should I find here but my neighbor and close friend." Lucy's eyes went right to Sheena, looked her up and down in less than a second and said, "Where are you two off to?"

"Nowhere, just giving my friend a tour of the neighborhood, that's all," Rex said as he stood there now enveloped in what was quickly turning into an uncomfortable silence.

"Hi, I'm Sheena. I think I saw you at the workshop?"

"Oh, right," Lucy said. "I didn't recognize you with your

clothes on and everything."

Rex wondered if anybody could hear them over the din of the TV and jukebox, decided that it if they were being overheard it was too late. "Yeah. Anyway, what are you doing?" Rex asked.

Lucy was already moving into his vacated seat and said, "Oh, nothing—meeting a friend for lunch and then watching the game. You two have fun now. Nice to see you again, Sheena."

Rex bit his lip and said, "Okay. See you later, Luce." He steered Sheena out the door and kept his arm on her elbow as they headed down the street.

"You're sure I'm not, um, intruding on anything between you?" Sheena said.

"No. I'm sure. We're just friends."

Rex escorted her through the front doors, her scent filling his head with lust. But his mind drifted back to the bar. Lucy was waiting for a friend; he and Sheena were now friends; Sheena was friends with François. It was such an odd word, encompassing so much, offering so much leeway while disguising true intentions, actions, implications, and feelings. Everybody was such good friends. He and his new friend stepped into the elevator, made their way down the hall passing through the door to Rex's inner sanctum. He offered her a drink as she dropped her purse and kicked her shoes off, becoming very comfortable, very fast. Rex pushed away any concerns about where all this was heading and what did it mean, if anything, as he locked the door.

He fixed them drinks, sat next to her on the couch, and waited for an opening, which didn't take long. He leaned over to kiss her on the lips. He pushed against her as she laid back and slid her tongue into his mouth. She was already writhing her hips as he peeled her top over her head, took her thin wrists in one hand and held them over her head. His mouth went to her pert breasts, sucking each nipple into pointed erections.

"Oh, god, sir. You're moving fast, aren't you?"

He used one hand to pop the snap on her jeans as he lightly bit her soft, warm belly. "Do you want me to stop?"

"What? No. Oh, god, don't stop."

He slid her jeans off, grabbed her panties and looked her in the eye. Seeing no trepidation, he slid them down in one motion, exposing what he had seen before at the workshop. But now she was here, under his total control. He licked a finger and teased her till she opened her legs. He remained fully clothed as he brought her to a quick climax, let her rest for moment and then encouraged her to move into the bedroom, her bare feet gently slapping the floor.

She flopped onto the bed on her stomach, her arms tucked beneath her. Rex slapped her naked bottom and said, "Up on all fours, Sheena." She obeyed, head down, tail up in a pose of total submission. "Don't move." Rex began to disrobe and pulled himself into full readiness. He spread her legs, rubbing between to make sure she was ready, before putting on a condom and slowly entering her while thinking about friends. Friends with benefits.

He chuckled to himself and began thrusting, slow and shallow at first, then gradually longer and deeper. She raised her upper half off the bed as he slid a hand up her back, along her spine, felt her thin, moist neck in his palm. He moved his hand farther up, burying his hand into her hair, tugging and pulling her head back, using it as a leverage point to slide his new friend forward and back, faster and faster till they both cried out in ecstasy and collapsed on the bed, panting.

"I thought we were going to play with the rope," Sheena said between breaths.

"Next time," Rex said.

CHAPTER 14

Sheena said some things after their play session that indicated she might be willing to spend the night, but Rex was concerned that they had already moved too far and too fast. He eased her out the door, promising to reconnect with her even though he was already having second thoughts. He muddled his way through the morning at work with his mind straying to what the cops found out about François and what he was going to do about the mysterious masked ball and the invite to the Coiled Whip.

If François was under arrest, Rex was off the hook with the Metro Police, which only left his ongoing yet somewhat intriguing dealings with Wellborn. If he could bring that to a close, he could get back to his somewhat normal life of worrying about something more mainstream, like dealing with back taxes and the IRS. Twice he picked up the phone to text something to Lucy but wasn't sure what he would say so he slid the phone into his pocket and headed out to lunch.

Wellborn was seated at his regular table poking at a cell phone as Rex entered and took a seat.

"Ahh, our man on the streets. How goes the mission, Mr. Armstrong?"

"Good question, Mr. Wellborn. Remind me again what I am

supposed to be finding out?"

Wellborn laughed a louder-than-necessary laugh, pulled an envelope out of his inside jacket pocket, and handed it to Rex.

As Rex took the envelope, Wellborn said, "You sir, are trying to befriend the mysterious François and determine if he is involving some of our trusted military leaders in what we in the business call 'espionage.' How is that going?"

"Right. Okay here's what I know. François's last name is Bellamy and he's pretty heavily involved in the local fetish scene, which last I heard is not illegal. I gave his name and his phone number to the local cops who want to talk to him about the murder of a girl named Amy, who was also involved in the scene and with whom I had a passing acquaintance with."

"Yes. You were one of the last people to see her alive, I believe."

"According to them. Anyway, François seems to know your generals, but I don't know in what context. Maybe he works for that French defense contractor you sent me to and it's all on the up and up. To be honest with you, I'm trying to remember how I got mixed up in all this stuff and wondering if I am now, as we say in the business, off on a wild goose chase."

Wellborn looked at him evenly. "I think the envelope in your possession will answer that question, but I'm sensing some doubt about your continued involvement. We believe you have made some progress in answering many questions we've had and hope that we can continue our arrangement."

"And who is 'we' again?"

"The 'we' doesn't matter at this point. It's so much alphabet soup."

"Yeah, well. I may be full of alphabet soup despite what's in the envelope or what's waiting for me behind door number two."

"And what about serving your country?"

"Seriously?" asked Rex, just as the waiter arrived.

They both ordered food and then resumed the conversation after the waiter was safely out of earshot.

Rex opened with, "I just can't believe that if this François guy, who appears to be some kind of European playboy with too much money, was trying to involve army generals in stealing drone technology, that you would send me, me who knows nothing about any of this stuff, to a shibari workshop in some goofy fetish club to uncover the secrets. None of this makes any sense. Couldn't you just tap their phones or hack their computers or get a real secret agent to do your dirty work?"

"All fair questions, Rex. First of all, government cutbacks have forced us to seek recruits outside our normal networks. Tapping the phone lines or hacking the computers of our own generals is at best politically incorrect these days and at worst illegal—not that I'm saying it hasn't been done, mind you. And you do…"

"Yeah, I know, I do fit a certain profile. You keep saying that."

"Only because it's true. Now, did you say, shibari?"

"Yeah, it's Japanese bondage with all these crazy ties and twists. Jesus, who can remember all that stuff? Talk about a weird fetish. I read it was developed by the Samurai."

"Quite correct, it borders on an art form, assuming you perceive creative knot tying as art."

"Wait. You know something about this stuff?"

"Only in passing. François was at this event? Did you see anybody who looked like the generals that you saw at the party?"

"François, yes. François's talky girlfriend, yes. Generals, no.

But since you have some passing knowledge in these things, maybe you know something about this," Rex said as he pulled the skeleton key out of his pocket and laid it on the table.

Wellborn eyes riveted to the key, and then he looked directly at Rex, who felt immediately uncomfortable.

"Where did you get that?" asked Wellborn.

"Why does everybody ask me that?"

"You've shown it to somebody else?"

"Yes. One of my sources, who shall remain nameless."

Wellborn picked the key up carefully, just as Chester had, and squinted at the logo. "Le Fouet Enroule. Well done, Mr. Armstrong. Have you been invited to join this fine association?" He gave the key back to Rex, using his hand to hide as much of the key as possible. "Put that back in your pocket and we would prefer you don't show it to any more of your sources."

"You know about this too? What the fuck? Who are these people and why do you know about them?"

Wellborn cleared his throat as the food arrived and dropped his napkin into his lap.

"We don't know much, as they are fond of secrecy. They are somewhat notorious for the activities they favor, but they are probably harmless in the bigger sense. Have they offered you membership?"

"No, but they did invite me to what sounds like a totally creepy party."

"What kind of creepy party?"

"I don't know. From what I've heard, it's heavy-duty S and M, which is not really my bag. Is it yours? Is that how you know about this? Is that what you're into?"

Wellborn began laughing so hard he had to put his fork down to compose himself and dabbed at the corners of his eyes with the napkin. "Oh, Mr. Armstrong, you never cease to surprise me."

"Well, I'm glad you find me amusing. But the thing is, these parties, everybody wears a mask. I think they've seen "*Eyes Wide Shut*" too many times."

"Or read the book the film was based on, which dates from the 1920s, I believe. Anyway, we would like you to attend the said party, observe and report back to us."

"You know what? This is really starting to sound like spying and I don't think it has anything to do with ripping off Metro or selling drone technology to the French or any of this other stuff. You're sounding creepier than the creeps. I'm going to have to say 'no' to this one."

"How about if we double your regular rate?"

Rex took a big bite of his sandwich and said, "No way. This isn't about the money. This goes way beyond money. This is not serving my country. This is the kind of stuff that's wrong with my country."

Wellborn hesitated for a second before turning to his salad with chunks of chicken breast, dressing on the side.

"I know this seems distasteful, Rex. But there could be information or activities happening at that event that could be of high value to us. Didn't you mention to me at one point that you were experiencing some difficulty with the IRS?" He looked at Rex while slowly turning the knife in his hand, the light glinting off the blade.

Rex dropped his sandwich and said, "Okay. You know what? That is really over the line. I don't know what you're talking about, I don't know who you actually are, who you work for or what. You're just some guy who turns up for lunch with a suit that matches his hat who keeps an office in an unmarked trailer in a school parking lot with a stack of cash in unmarked envelopes. I'm still saying no. Get yourself another monkey in a mask for this crazy scheme."

"As you wish, Rex," Wellborn said. They finished the meal in an uncomfortable silence before Rex exited with a wave.

Rex was pissed off, frustrated and bugged by the whole deal. Despite his mixed feelings about the scene, spying on the participants for an as yet to be named federal agency seemed wrong no matter how you sliced it. He was stomping back toward the office thinking evil thoughts about the regular people who were crowding the sidewalks and staring up at street signs. Why couldn't he be more like them? Just regular folks lost in the big city looking at the sights. The office was close to the National Mall, so clots of tourists regularly showed up in the neighborhood trying to find the Museum of American Art or Fords Theater. He put his head down, navigated around a crew in matching T-shirts, and felt his phone vibrate in his pocket. "Now what do you want?" he said to himself. He pulled it out and felt a quick sense of panic and arousal when he noticed a message was from Sheena.

"Hoping you're having a great day. I had a ball yesterday ☺"

He smiled to himself, resisting the urge to answer, and slid the phone back into his pocket. He muddled through the rest of the day, went home, did laundry, and reopened the invitation to the Coiled Whip party. There was nothing on it about wearing masks, who he could bring or where it was being held. Maybe all that would be provided, if and when he responded. He put the computer to sleep and went down to check the mail, hoping there wouldn't be any but was disappointed.

He stood over the counter in the apartment building mailroom, dropping junk mail into the trash slot until he came to an official-looking envelope from the IRS that looked very serious. "Goddamn it," Rex said. He tore open the envelope flashing on the words that were demanding payment from him and threatening garnishment, interest, and penalties. "Fuck me."

He sulked back into the elevator, rode it upstairs and poured himself a stiff drink, already knowing the booze wasn't going to offer any help with his tax issues. He picked up the letter, along with a few other pieces of late notices from bill collectors, and flung them toward the window. The envelopes caught wind and by turns dove and swooped their way across the room until gravity forced them to the carpet.

There was a knock at the door and Rex heard himself yell, "What?" a bit too loudly for a multi-unit apartment building. He ignored the knock, took a healthy swig of hooch, and pretended that he was having a bad dream, but there was another knock. "Goddamn these people, what the fuck?" He went to the door, flipped the lock open and without bothering to check the peephole, threw the door wide open to see the cops.

"You've got to be fucking kidding me. Oh, this is perfect. Come on in guys, and do not, repeat, do not ask me if I'm here alone, okay?" Detectives Span and Franklin entered the space, their eyes automatically going to opposite corners of the room. Franklin nonchalantly said, "You here alone, Mr. Armstrong?"

Rex slumped down into a chair at the kitchen table, put his hands over his face and said, "No, Detective, there's a whole platoon of Isis members and inner city thugs in the bedroom, along with some secret agents hiding in the closet. They've all been waiting patiently for you to show up and now, they shall emerge and pounce. Come on out, fellows, the five-oh is here!"

"You are a funny, funny, man, Rex. So funny I forgot to laugh," said Franklin as he noticed the mail scattered around the living room. "Catching up on your bills, are we?"

"What do you guys want? Is it against the law to throw mail in your living room now?"

"Not that we're aware of," Span said. He moved toward Rex, pulling something from his coat pocket. "Have you ever seen this before?" A black Nokia phone in a baggie dangled in front of his nose.

"No, detective. That's obviously a cell phone that doesn't belong to me. Why are you asking?"

"Because the number on the business card you gave us rings to this phone."

"Okay, so where is the person that owns that phone?" asked Rex.

"We were hoping you could tell us," said Span.

Rex returned his face to his hands. "Aren't you guys supposed to be the detectives? I gave you the number, you found the phone, so who belongs to the phone? How should I know? That's your job, isn't it?"

Franklin slid the chair next to Rex out more roughly than he needed to and plopped down next to him, his face edging in close enough for Rex to smell his breath, which reeked of chilidogs and onions.

"I think we discussed job duties last time we were here, and we don't need to go over all that again. So here's the deal. We found the phone in a magazine rack in a newsstand in Union Station. The number is registered to a guy named Mohammed Shalaki, speaking of Isis. Only thing is, Mohammed doesn't really seem to exist. No social security number, no driver's license, no real identity at all, which is weird, since it actually seems to be a real name. So apparently the name and number that you gave us appear to be fabricated, which makes you a suspect for aiding and abetting, impeding an ongoing homicide investigation, and possible accessory after the fact, which kind of explains why we are here, again knocking on your door, now basking in your sparkling charm and asking you, where is your pal, François Bellamy or Mohammed or whatever his name is? You remember François, don't you? He was the guy that was even a better suspect than you, right? Isn't that what you told us? Except he doesn't seem to exist, see?"

"Did you try running a check on François Bellamy, Officer Dipshit? To see where that trail might lead?"

Franklin's forearm launched toward Rex's throat, pushing his head into the wall with a loud thunk. The chair legs squeaked. Rex felt his throat closing from the force that the detective was now applying to his neck. Rex was in an awkward position, still seated but pinned against the wall, his arm useless under the table and being held in place by Franklin's other hand.

Rex instinctively held his breath, narrowed his gaze and looked into Franklin's face, which was registering no emotion whatsoever. Franklin would have been perfectly happy to choke Rex into unconsciousness or even kill him without a second thought. "Classic sadist," Rex thought to himself. He wished the blow had come with more warning because he didn't have the chance to take a full breath of air and already felt himself starting to gag and choke.

He fought the urge back as flashes of light began to appear in the corners of his vision. Things had already started to go black. Rex thought he heard the door open. A familiar voice asked, "Hey! What's going on in here?" Rex felt the pressure on his throat subside. He gagged and coughed as he pulled himself into a more upright position.

"Rex, are you okay?" Lucy said. Rex turned his head to see his neighbor who had now rescued him from the cops, twice. "Fuck," he said under his breath. "Yes, I'm fine. Detective Franklin and I were just having a wrestling match and lucky for him you came in when you did. I was about to use my reverse sleeper hold maneuver."

Franklin was now towering over him, breathing a bit hard, straightening his jacket, and reaching into his wallet for a business card. "Here's the deal, Sexy Rexy. You find us François toot-sweet or you are going to be a guest at the DC jail for a while. You know what happens to good-looking white boys like you in there? Oh, wait. You might actually enjoy that kind of thing. We're going for the warrant right now. If you have any kinky rabbits up your sleeve, now would be a good time to pull one out." Franklin flipped the business card at him as he and Span nodded at Lucy and left the room.

"Oh my god, Rex. Are you all right?"

"No," Rex said, "I am not right at all."

"What the hell is happening? Were those the two cops from the other night?"

Rex rubbed his throat, felt for damaged cartilage, and made a shallow, dry, coughing sound. "They couldn't find François. They only found his phone, so now they think I'm their best lead in this thing. It's really frustrating. I hardly knew this damn Amy chick. "I never slept with her, and I'm going to end up taking the rap for something I know nothing about."

"Well, actually you do know something, don't you, Rex?"

He pulled himself to his feet and reached for the whiskey bottle. "What are you talking about?"

"I'm talking about this scene thing that you're mixed up in, which seems to be full of creeps and other demented types. The cops are hassling you because it looks freaky, Rex, and you are the only freak they know."

Rex took the cap off the bottle and threw it across the room. He thought about a story he'd heard about Russians who would uncork a bottle of vodka and throw the cap away, declaring their intentions to empty the bottle in one sitting. Maybe he just needed to get a good drunk on. He ignored the concept of a glass, took a mighty swig from the bottle, brushed the excess liquor off his lips with the back of his hand and said, "Yeah, well, I know where all the freaks will be this weekend, and everybody wants to know about them. The feds, the cops, and the pervos all want to see what happens behind the doors of the Coiled Whip society."

"What the hell are you talking about? You're really starting to concern me."

Rex felt the acid wash of the booze slaking its way down his throat, his chest and neck already warming from the touch of ethanol, adding to the irritation from the choking.

He was on his feet, arms held wide, his voice cracking and rising within the confines of the room. "Be not afraid, Lucy dear, for I am not dead nor imprisoned yet. For I shall attend this lurid event that causes brave men to shake in their boots. I shall go to unmask the killer, satisfy the curiosity of the cat in the hat, and keep my sweet ass out of jail. And you, my faithful rescuer and neighbor…perhaps you will want to go with me. Accompany me into the belly of the beast, so I as yet may be redeemed."

Rex took another drink from the bottle and slumped onto the couch, not really caring any more about whether he should go or who he should he take. He felt himself on a conveyor belt of indecision, riding toward where he was supposed to be and doing what he was supposed to do. But rather than riding along complacently and submissively waiting for something to happen, he now knew what he had to do. The time of self-destruction was over, not counting the bottle in his hand, of course. It was time to stand up, get a grip, grab the wheel, put on the belt and hit the gas. Otherwise, these fuckers were going to eat him alive, like a pack of wolves.

CHAPTER 15

Rex thanked Lucy for another timely rescue and eased her out the door before the questions went toward what happened between he and Sheena, which he didn't want to answer. He continued to work his way through the bottle, but slowing his descent as he turned on the computer and navigated back to the invitation to the Coiled Whip party. He clicked on a button that said "Attend" which opened up another dialog box that asked him for the number on his key.

"What the fuck? What number?" He found the key on top of his dresser and located a small magnifying glass in his desk. He turned on the desk lamp, squinted at the key and, sure enough, on the end that went into the lock, he found the numbers "777" stamped into the metal. "Triple sevens has to be lucky," Rex said to the walls. He punched in the digits. The computer spun and clicked for a few beats and then another screen appeared entitled "Le Fouet Enroule—The Rules."

"Here we go," Rex said, "let see what the deal is." He was anxious and curious to see the Eurostyle of doing things, wondering if they really did have a classier take on things.

"Le Fouet Enroule—The Rules."

1.   Congratulations. A friend of great import has bestowed upon you a wonderful gift. You are now a probationary member of a

secret society made up of individuals hand-selected from the worlds of wealth, power and sensory exploration. Rest assured you will be given every courtesy and paid the greatest of respects as long as you remain true to the rules. Any infraction can cause immediate dismissal, so rule number 1 is to read and abide by the rules.

2.   You will not discuss the activities or communications of the group with anyone outside the group.

3.   There are no observers in the group. If you attend a sanctioned event you are required to actively participate by volunteering to serve in one of the theme rooms for the minimum of one hour.

4.   All normal scene rules that you are used to, including non-interference in ongoing scenes, getting proper consent, personal hygiene, safe protocols of physical contact, excessive use of alcohol or drugs, use of safe words, etc., also apply to the group. Leave any bad habits you may possess outside the door.

5.   You may bring one guest with you. Guests are not required to participate in the theme rooms. To retain proper balance of the sexes, a guest must be the opposite sex of you. They must remain masked at all times during a sanctioned event. It is forbidden to share event location addresses or other contact information with guests. Guests may apply to become members using the standard procedure.

6.   Attending any sanctioned group event automatically waives your rights regarding any type of legal action. Play safe and play at your own risk.

7.   For all sanctioned events, members and guest are required to wear masks that completely hide their identity. Removing your mask or any other's mask is grounds for immediate dismissal.

8.   The event you've been invited to will be devoted to the following themes. If you wish to attend, pick a theme and sign in to claim a time slot by clicking here. The word "here" was a link that took him to a chart of one-hour time slots for the themes labeled, "Wife Whipping, At Her Feet, Sissy Boys, Edge Play, Dungeon."

"Holy shit," Rex said to himself.

There was really only one group he felt he could comfortably fit into, so he clicked on the "Dungeon" link, which asked to identify himself as "Master" or "Slave." He clicked on "Master," volunteered for the 9: 00-time slot, and hit "Accept." Another dialog box opened and told him to expect an email with the exact location of the party and the protocol for gaining entry.

Questions immediately popped into his brain, fighting their way through the haze of alcohol. Was François working one of the rooms at the last party? There wasn't a shibari theme listed, maybe they changed them on a regular basis? Edge play was a broad term, was it fire, needles, breath control? Would he arouse suspicion if he showed up with no guest? Was Sheena too skittish to go back if he were to ask her? Would François be taking her?

He ignored the questions and texted Wellborn saying he might be changing his mind but he wanted four times the usual rate. Two thousand dollars could go a long way toward keeping the IRS off his back for a while. Wellborn immediately texted back, "Done! But we want to know if the generals are there, especially Hap."

Rex bit his tongue and then yelled at the empty room, "Everybody wears a mask, Wellborn! How the hell am I supposed to identify Hap? But you know what? Who gives a shit? This is all smoke and mirror bullshit, anyway, so, sure, I'll identify your kinked-up, traitorous general for you, Wellborn. Just let old Rex handle it for you. After all, I'm a freaking secret agent freak, working for Uncle Sam." He finished his verbal tirade and texted back, "Done!" Next, he found Detective Franklin's business card and keyed in the number, which took him to voicemail.

"Hello, Detective. This is your favorite punching bag, Rex Armstrong. I have on good authority that François will be at a kink party this Saturday night at a secret location that is being emailed to me very shortly. Once I have the location I will turn it over to you, and hopefully, you and Detective Span will accompany me to this sordid little event so you can bust François, close your case on

Amy, and perhaps meet a nice masochist so you two can live happily ever after. If, on the other hand, you throw my ass in jail, as you're so excited to do, I may not be able to access my email and therefore will not know the secret location or the secret password to get in and therefore none of us will be able to attend. Please standby."

Rex hung up, chuckled a little to himself and took another swig. He texted Lucy, "Any plans for Saturday night? I'd like to take you on a date."

Then he clicked the phone off and found his cigarettes. Suddenly feeling lighter and in more control, he went out onto the balcony to smoke.

CHAPTER 16

Lucy didn't reply that night nor had she replied by the next morning, but Rex wasn't that concerned. He figured he could always attend the party by himself, which might be the smarter way to handle it. There was also no reply from the cops, and he felt himself looking over his shoulder from time to time as he walked from the train to the office. He did get a text from Sheena asking him how his day was going, which boosted his ego and caused some consternation at the same time.

The last time they got together she seemed to be much less talkative. She had a hot body and she was into the kink scene, so why couldn't she be a candidate for the coveted position of his future ex-wife? Was there a true lack of spark between them, or should the kindling be given a chance to flame up before discounting the possibilities? He texted her back and casually asked what she had planned for the weekend, partially because he was curious about whether she would be attending the Coiled Whip party and partially because he wanted to take another ride with her, but this time with more accessories.

Rex wiled away the hours at work and checked his personal In-Box several times, looking for the secret party details he'd been promised. So far, nothing. He pinged Chester to see if he was going to be out and about anytime soon, as he wanted to compare notes about the Coiled Whipsters with somebody who seemed to know something about them besides Wellborn. He also texted

Wellborn asking when he could pick up his down payment for the upcoming assignment. As usual, Wellborn was the most efficient responder and suggested they meet for lunch on Friday at the usual spot, usual time.

Chester was the next to reply and indicated he'd be available for a Happy Hour get-together as long as Rex was buying. They agreed on a place. Rex plowed through the rest of the day and walked toward the meeting, again looking over his shoulder for the coppers. Chester had selected a dive bar a few blocks from the agency where the bartenders knew them both. Chester was already at the bar with a stout in front of him when Rex came and took the stool next to him.

"Hello, mate, been here long?" asked Rex.

"I left my place right after you called. I've had twelve beers and told Andy to put them all on your tab."

"You're a very funny man. How's tricks?"

Chester took a sip of stout and said, "When I'm lucky, the tricks come with treats. When I'm unlucky. I just get tricked. What's new with you? Any new developments with the you-know-whos?"

"Funny you should ask, I got an invite to a masked soiree happening this very Saturday. Will you be in attendance?"

"I will not sir, as they are not my kind of crowd."

"And that surprises me, Chester. I mean, here you are, an out-and-about fetish club owner, businessman, entrepreneur…a promoter of the lifestyle. And yet you and they do not mix well. Can you explain that to me?"

The conversation was paused as Andy, the bartender, greeted Rex, took his order and returned shortly with a pilsner.

"You've hit the nail straightaway, Rexy. I am out and they are not. I promote; they guard their privacy—and that's okay.

Although we live in the same world, our homes are on opposite sides of town."

"I see. It turns out, I'm invited to visit them in a secret location, which has yet to be revealed."

"Mmm-hmm. How about money? Have they mentioned the membership fee?"

"You know what? No. There has been no mention of that, which is surprising, right? I mean have you ever gone to an event where there wasn't some kind of a charge?"

"Oh, they will ask. Assuming you pass your audition, you'll be asked to become a full-fledged member, which means thousands of dollars, old chap. Not twenty bucks here, twenty bucks there."

"Thousands?"

"Thousands. And there will be a fairly persuasive sales pitch like you were considering a timeshare but with whips and chains in the basement."

"I see. That's easy because I don't have thousands. The other thing is they require everybody attending to participate in one of the activities. Apparently, observers aren't welcome."

"Quite right. They want everybody involved in case something heads south."

"What do you mean, heads south?"

Chester took another sip and looked over his shoulder, which caused Rex to look in that direction, too.

"It's like I told you before, mate. People have been known to get hurt at these things. I mean seriously injured. Of course, they'll have you sign the standard waiver but they go a step farther to make sure everybody participates. Nobody can say, 'Oh, I was there, but I was just watching,' right?" Everybody is responsible, everybody is at risk."

"You're taking all the fun out of it, Chester."

"Yeah, well, that depends on your idea of fun, doesn't it? Are you taking a female companion and have you picked out your masks yet?"

"No, but I was thinking of going as Ronald Reagan."

Chester choked a bit on his beer, brushed some spilled drops off his chin with a napkin and said, "That's very funny. There's a costume shop on Capitol Hill they all like. A bit overpriced and theatrical, but I think the guy who runs it is in the scene or is at least a supplier of props."

"I know the place," Rex said. "I'll check it out. Haven't decided on a date yet, but I have two candidates in mind."

"Yeah, well, I would recommend taking the one who is the least squeamish, because it's going to get nasty. Did they ask you to volunteer for a position on the team?"

"Dungeon master."

"Perfect. Shall we have another?"

"Absolutely." Rex motioned for a refill. "Do you know anything about when they divulge the secret location or where it might be?"

"I think they change it on a regular basis, but it will probably be somewhere remote. The person who actually owns the space will be a bit of a mystery and you won't be notified until the last minute—usually the day of the event."

"Seriously?"

"Quite serious, and as dungeon master it will be your responsibility to make sure that everybody plays nice and to properly torture anybody who turns up without a torturer."

"Nice."

"And of course you'll have dibs torturing your own guest."

"Well, of course. You sure you're not going?"

"Quite sure, but I wish you the best of luck. Do you think these sick bastards have anything to do with the demise of sweet Amy?"

"I do, and I hope to shed some light on that mystery, which will hopefully get the Metro Police Department off my back and keep me out of jail."

They finished their second round and Rex considered staying for a third but then thought better of it. He said farewell to Chester and wandered back toward the Metro station.

The rest of the week unspooled as anonymous days spilled into each other. Rex felt like he was crawling through mud, and he was still anxious about the cops showing up where he least expected them. He found himself avoiding his regular haunts, taking alternative routes to work and passing through the back exit to his apartment. Lucy eventually did respond to his inquiry, but Rex couldn't bring himself to text in the details of his request. It all sounded too sordid and far-fetched like he was sleepwalking through a dream that he couldn't wake from. He was also purposely vague and distant with Sheena, the aching in his loins prompting him to re-open the dialogue, but the feeling of dread in his soul stopping him from punching in the words.

He also ignored the mailbox and any more bad news that might be waiting for him there. Calling his ex was out of the question. He tried to distract himself by thinking about what would be a good costume for a dungeon master. Something that would conceal his identity, inspire respect from this particular crowd of freaks and make him feel confident in carrying out his duties. He considered something comical to show that it was all in good fun, some kind of campy rubber mask or perhaps a dark hood of some sort that would still conceal his face.

He Googled "Illuminati masked balls" and saw weird, gold-faced creatures, Victorian-influenced costumes, and people wearing animal heads. It all seemed rather silly and he wished he would have gotten more direction from Chester. But since he'd never been to one, what did he really know about it?

He forced himself out of the apartment, leaving the back way and then trudged up to the costume shop. There were all kinds of superhero replicas, and pre-packaged archetypes of pirates, cowboys, and pop culture icons. He tried to picture himself in the shop with Sheena or Lucy, picking something out as a couple off for an adventure into the forbidden, but he was drawing a complete blank. The guy behind the counter was reading a book that Rex couldn't see the title of and he didn't seem to be at all interested in Rex's presence.

What did he want to be? Who did he want to represent himself as? What was the proper tone for the whole thing? The go-to standard was the hooded, leather-clad dominant with some leather armbands, high boots, muscle shirt, vest and all the accouterments. Gah. He wanted something that was out of the ordinary but at the same time would fit in. He flipped through the racks and found a simple paper mask that covered the whole face. There were eyeholes, a small opening for the mouth, and two holes for the nostrils.

Upon further inspection, Rex realized this was a customizable blank designed to be painted and have things attached to it. There was one elastic string to hold it on—the picture of simplicity. It was cheap and could be easily removed should the need arise. It was a somewhat anonymous, open to interpretation and at the same time—quite creepy, like a mime or a clown without any expression or emotional interaction. Perfect. Rex bought two, ignored the props and went home, once again entering from the rear of the building and looking over his shoulder.

He stepped into the elevator, punched in his floor, and was about to breathe a sigh of relief as the doors started to close. "Hold it!" someone yelled, and he jumped. He saw a familiar hand as

Lucy stepped inside.

"Well, well, well, if it isn't the mysterious Rex Armstrong. What's going on, missing neighbor of mine?" she asked.

"I'm not missing; I'm right here."

"I can see that. When you ask a young lady such as myself out for a date, it's good to follow up and provide said lady with the appropriate details so she can make an informed decision. Oh, is this your floor?"

"Yes, it is. Would you like to join me for a drink where I will divulge said details?"

"I'd love to, unfortunately, I'm otherwise engaged."

The door opened as Rex felt his hopes fall. "I know, I'm sorry. I'm kind of going back and forth on some stuff so I haven't been totally forthcoming."

He laid his hand against the elevator door to keep it from closing, which caused it to start softly bonging a warning. "I need to get this thing resolved with the cops and it looks like the only way that's going to happen is to go to another one of these events to find the French guy."

"François? We're still doing that?"

"Yes. Has he contacted you?"

"I don't know, I haven't looked at my email. I'm too busy leading what we normal people call 'a life.' You might consider getting yourself one at some point. Now if you'll excuse me, I have to go tidy up a bit." The elevator bonged again, this time sounding more insistent.

"Right, sure. But about Saturday?"

"Call me tomorrow, Rex. As in, call me on the phone and we will have what's called a 'conversation' about it. Okay?"

"Okay. How about we meet for a drink or something?"

"Call me. Tomorrow. On the phone. Bye."

Rex stepped off not looking behind him and wondered if he actually had Lucy's number—then realized he had to since he texted her all the time. He hated talking on the phone socially; it always seemed so unfocused and random. He went home, double-locked the door and tried on his mask with some of his normal, scene-friendly clothes. As the look began to emerge, he felt better about things. He toyed with the idea of drawing some sinister eyebrows or facial hair onto the mask. He thought he kept hearing movement in the hallways and frequently peered through the keyhole expecting to see Span and Franklin with a pair of handcuffs in their hand and brutality in their eyes. But each time, the hallway was empty.

He went to bed early, tossing and turning, flopping around in the bed like a fish out of water. He wrote the cause off to anxiety and eventually drifted off to sleep. He woke the next morning, dreading the phone call to Lucy but unsure why. He waited till after work, poured himself a stiff drink and took a fresh pack of smokes out to the balcony. He dialed without thinking too hard about what he was going to say and felt a mix of relief and disappointment wash over him as the call went to voicemail.

"Hey, Luce, it's Rex, calling you as you requested. I'm home if you want to come down, or I can come up. Call me back when you get this. Still really torn about this deal on Saturday. Anyway, I'm around if you're available to 'chat.'"

He hung up and instantly regretted using the word chat – it sounded kind girly and overly formal. There was a knock on the door and he jumped. He walked silently over to it and looked out the peephole but couldn't see anything—like maybe somebody had a big fat cop thumb over the lens on the other side. He instantly reached for the doorknob but then stopped. Did they know he was in here? How could they know? Maybe he was out. Would they try to break it down or ask the front desk to let them in? Did they really have a search warrant? Maybe it was Lucy's thumb on the hole. He waited silently, now aware of the sounds of his own breathing.

The knocking started again. A bit louder and a bit more insistent as Rex jumped involuntarily. He peeped through again, but it was dark. Maybe it wasn't even the cops. Somebody playing a trick on him?

Then the phone started ringing. Rex wrapped his hands around it and turned away from the door, bumbling around trying to find the button to silence it. He turned down the volume, looked to see who it was, and it was Lucy. Was she standing outside the door, calling him? He walked to the balcony and hit the answer key just as the ringing stopped. He slapped the phone against his thigh, muffled a curse and heard his door close behind him. He spun around, stepped back inside and saw Franklin and Span standing in his apartment—again.

"How'd you guys get in here? You can't come in here. That's breaking and entering or something, isn't it?" Rex said. He noticed how stressed his own voice was sounding. He thought about bringing up the question of a search warrant but on second thought, he didn't really want to know.

"Actually, Mr. Armstrong, your door was open and we thought we heard sounds of a struggle," said Span.

"Sounds of a struggle? What sounds? There wasn't any struggle. As you can see, once again I am here alone, minding my own business."

"Minding your own business, huh? Well that's a switch, isn't it, Detective Span?" Franklin said. He was reaching behind him and now produced a pair of handcuffs. "What did we tell you was going to happen if you didn't help us crack this little caper, Rexy? Ready to go up to D Street Southeast and meet some of your new playmates? I hear there's a nice view of the Anacostia from up there."

Span took a step toward him as Rex held up his hands. "Hang

on a second. Did you guys get my voicemail? I called that number you gave me and left a message about what's going on. It's happening Saturday night. You can go with me if you want. I don't care anymore."

Franklin stopped, put a hand on his hip and acted like he was trying to remember something. "You know what? I do remember getting a message from you—where you said something about me meeting a nice masochist or something like that. I think he was trying to insult me, Detective Span. Was that how you heard it?"

Span offered no reaction, his face blank as Franklin resumed closing in on Rex, a soft, half-step at a time, anticipating what Rex might do to avoid him.

"That was a joke. I was kidding you. Just a joke. Listen, François is going to be at this party Saturday night. I want you guys to go with me as a back up. You know? We'll find the French guy. Maybe you can match some DNA from him or whatever and boom! Case closed. I go back to my silly life. Deal?"

Rex's phone beeped, signaling him that someone had left him a voicemail. He looked down for a second to check the screen and felt his arm being twisted behind his back. His hand immediately went numb as he heard the phone fall and hit the floor.

"Ow, fuck!" Rex said as he went onto his toes, trying to create some space and relieve the pain of his arm being forced up toward the ceiling, but the force just increased.

"Now you listen to me, you fucking freak. I am really tired of the games. Understand? Give us the address of this little gathering, which is probably another fucking lie out your mouth, and we will handle who's backing up who."

"Gahhh. I don't have the address yet," Rex said through clenched teeth. "They don't give it out till the last minute. I probably won't know till Friday. That's how they always do it."

"And what if you're lying? Or what if you don't get the address or the French guy doesn't show up? Then what happens?"

"Ow! Shit. I'll turn myself in. I'll come downtown, you can question me or whatever you want to do. Full cooperation..."

"How about a confession, Rex? Want to sign a piece of paper saying you did it and we can end this right now?"

He didn't think his arm could be forced any higher and yet Franklin kept pushing it up. A new wave of pain washed over him.

"Oh, god…I didn't kill her…can't sign a…" He felt himself starting to black out as the world went blurry and the lights started to dance. The pain suddenly stopped and he felt himself on the floor, his nose on the carpet. He thought for a second that he might throw up as he struggled to push himself into a sitting position.

Franklin's standing form was backlit and hazy as Rex watched the cop straighten his jacket, made a gesture to Span and then they moved out of his sight. He heard the door slam and they were gone. He laid on the floor for awhile, waiting for the feeling to return to his fingers and wondering about permanent nerve damage. It was a risk when tying people up, he was sure it was a risk when forcing human limbs into positions they weren't supposed to go.

He thought about calling the DC Metro Police Department and filing a complaint against Detective Franklin for excessive force and trespassing. He'd moved past fear and resentment and now contemplated behavior born from anger and physical anguish.

He found his phone, checked it for damage and was relieved that was intact and working. He punched the voicemail button and heard this from Lucy, "Okay, calling you back. I don't think this thing on Saturday is a good idea, Rex. I like you, but it's all a bit crazy for me, you know? Call me back when you get this if you feel up to it."

Rex decided he didn't feel up to it. She would just think he was even crazier if the told her what had just happened. He found his smokes, freshened his drink, swallowed three Tylenols and went to the balcony until he felt numb enough to sleep. He was still sore the next day, but his mind was fairly clear.

He had a productive morning and arrived on time for lunch with Wellborn, who as usual, was already seated. He was reading a copy of *The Los Angeles Times*.

"What's the news from La-La Land Rona Barrett?"

"All is well, Mr. Armstrong. Please join me."

The hat was on one chair and Rex took the one directly across from Wellborn, who dropped the paper and looked him over.

"So. Do we have a location for the event tomorrow?"

Rex dropped the napkin in his lap and said, "We do not, sir. Still waiting for the secret location to be revealed."

"How exciting," Wellborn said. He reached into his jacket and pulled out the plain white envelope. "And what about the local policemen? Have they been around to see you?"

"As a matter of fact, they have. One of them tried to remove my arm last night. Luckily I passed out just as he was about to complete the maneuver."

"What did you tell them?"

"I told them the same thing I'm telling you. I don't know where the stupid party is happening because the stupid people running it haven't sent out the stupid location yet."

"Sounds, um, stupid," Wellborn said as he handed the envelope across the table.

"Really stupid and here's another thing I just thought of. Suppose this little affair isn't even in the District of Columbia? Sheena told me she went to one of these things and it was 'out in the sticks.' If we're going to the burbs, these cops aren't going to be to follow me, will they? Isn't there some kind of jurisdictional cop thing that prevents them crossing the city line?"

"I'm sure you're right, Rex, but I wouldn't worry about it. That's their problem. But for your own safety, I would recommend keeping them in the loop, as we say."

"Gee thanks. What are you having? Something sensible like the chicken or fish?"

"Haven't decided. Maybe a big juicy burger."

"Finally we're talking the same language."

"Are you planning on attending the event with an escort?"

"No. I'll probably go by myself. This whole thing is so weird I don't want to mix anybody up in it."

"Understood. Have you chosen a theme yet?"

Rex felt his brain suddenly hit a brick wall as he body froze into position. "Did I tell you about the themes when we texted the other night?" Rex started to reach for his phone to answer his own question but stopped himself. He thought he saw Wellborn's eyebrow jump the slightest amount but maybe it was just a natural movement.

"No, we didn't talk about the themes, Rex, but we do have some knowledge of this group and how they like to operate. There's usually themed rooms and of course, the masks. Who are you going as?"

"A kinky mime," Rex said, which caused Wellborn to laugh louder than what Rex considered normal.

"I'm glad you find my costume choice amusing. The whole thing sounds very silly to me. And speaking of silly, how am I supposed to recognize whoever I'm supposed to be looking for if everybody is wearing a mask?"

"You're looking for the generals. Especially Hap. He's not hard to spot due to his physical size. Tall, barrel-chested, moves like somebody who has spent most of his life in the military. Plus,

I think you'll notice that some of the costumes are not as concealing as you might think. We're interested in Hap interacting with François or anybody else that may be speaking a foreign language, especially if they are speaking French. You don't speak, French, do you, Rex?"

"I do not, and you've already asked me that but I've always loved their fries."

This caused Wellborn to burst out laughing again, which Rex found amusing, as he didn't think it was that funny. He eventually calmed down, wiping the corner of his eyes with a napkin. "Oh, you are a funny man. The last thing I want to tell you is, watch your back when you're leaving the party. If anything violent is going to happen, that is when I would expect it."

Rex looked across the table at his lunch companion, who was now slowly twisting the butter knife around and around in his fingers as he gave Rex a long, even look in the eye. Again the killer stare, or was it just his overactive imagination? He really couldn't get a straight read on this guy. The rest of the lunch was uneventful and Rex walked out, patting the envelope of cash in his jacket pocket. He finished the rest of the day at work, left on time, and headed back to the apartment feeling relaxed and upbeat.

He walked through the front door, pressed the "up" button on the elevator and felt his heart stop as the doors opened to reveal Lucy, who was still dressed in her power suit from work. She must have been coming up from the parking garage.

"Wow," Rex said as he stepped in and pushed the button for his floor.

"I'm assuming that's a good wow," Lucy said.

"You look great, girlfriend."

"Oh, why thank you, Rex. How come you never called me back?"

"You know, you were a very good sport for going with me last time, but the whole thing made me uncomfortable. So I didn't want to put you through it again."

The elevator bonged, announcing his floor as the doors slid open.

"If I went with you, would it help get you out of this mess?" Lucy's polished fingernail stabbed the "hold door" button. They were done in a tasteful blue, matching her suit. She looked Rex in the eye.

"Well, it would be good to have another pair of eyes at this thing but I don't want to—"

"Shhh," Lucy said. "Is there more tying up and that kind of thing scheduled?"

"Actually it's more of a torture chamber this time, but I'm in charge of the dungeon for an hour, so I could torture you very lightly."

Her eyes narrowed as she tried to read his face. "Sounds heavenly. What's the dress code?" she asked.

"Black, skimpy, tight, dungeony. Plus you have to wear a mask. I have an extra one you could borrow." The elevator began bonging about being held against its will.

"What time and how would we get there?" she asked.

"I would pick you up at eight and we would ride the bike," he said.

She pursed her lips, looked at him and leaned in, "I'm in, Rex. But this is the last time. Comprendo?" Then she kissed him quickly on the lips and stepped out.

The doors closed as Rex said, "Holy shit."

CHAPTER 17

Rex twisted the throttle on the motorcycle and felt the rush of acceleration as he and Lucy headed out toward suburbia. The location of the event had finally been revealed and he used the GPS app on his phone to guide him into the wilds of Montgomery County—an area outside of Silver Spring that he'd never been to. He could feel Lucy hands around his waist holding on as the machine plummeted down the back roads he'd chosen as the preferred route.

He'd texted Span and Franklin the address and promised to share whatever he learned at the evening festivities. He'd also texted Sheena, telling her that he was going to be tied up for the weekend but promising to get back in touch after it was over. Rex had an idea of what to expect at the party, but he was anxious about the unknowns that wouldn't reveal themselves until it was too late to do anything about them. His mental state veered around between anger, excitation, trepidation, and concern that he was getting deeper into a situation that had only become worse with each new development. This would have to end it for him, one way or another.

What seemed like an unending series of twists and turns took them into a subdivision of McMansions that seemed to be under construction but at the same time, deserted. As fortunes in Washington improved for many, the suburbs had continued to expand out into a network of far-reaching cul-de-sacs. Night was falling. Rex squinted into the tiny map on his phone, which seemed to dead end somewhere very close to where they were. There were streets of empty houses around them, some looked nearly complete, others still under construction. At some point, the sidewalks, street signs, and curbs stopped. They were rolling over barely paved roads heading toward a house removed from the others, standing off by itself. It was clearly older than the new ones filling in the neighborhood and looked to be an old farmhouse— probably the central building for all the acreage they'd just rode through. It was still here for some reason, standing inside a partially pulled-down wire fence and guarded by what used to be a gate. In the place of a gate was a black Chevy Suburban that was parked and blocking the entrance.

"Here we go," Rex said over his shoulder. He wasn't sure Lucy could even hear him as they were both wearing full-face helmets, which would help hide their identities until they could get off the bike and put their masks on. Rex pulled up to the vehicle and pointed his front wheel at the midsection of the Suburban.

A very nondescript looking white dude wearing a dark suit and an earpiece stepped out of the vehicle and walked up to Rex.

"Yes, sir, can we help you?"

Rex flipped the eye screen up. "Yes, I'm here for the event."

"What event is that, sir?"

"The event that I was invited to. You guys sent me the location."

"Okay, well there is a private party going on for the future residents of the community here, but all of our guests have already checked in. Are you sure you have the right location?"

The guy in the suit touched his earpiece as Rex felt his anger rising, "Look, I got an invite, okay. This is the address you sent me, even though there really isn't an address here that I can see. Do you have a list or something? Can you check to see if I'm on the list?"

"There is no list, sir, and as I say all of our people are already here. Maybe you have the wrong date?" The suit guy repositioned himself so his hands were in front of him, preparing for some kind of confrontation, as Rex thought about getting off the bike as gracefully as possible and punching his lights out. He took a breath and said, "It's tonight, okay? I know what day it is. You guys sent me the location. You gave me a goddamn key, all right?"

The suit seemed to stop for a second and his head cocked slightly. "You say you have a key, sir?"

Rex started fumbling in his pockets and said, "Yes, of course, I have a key." He found it, pulled it out and handed it to the suit guy. "Does this help?"

The guy took the key, cocked an eyebrow and said, "Quite a bit, sir. Give me a moment, won't you?" He took the key and turned his back giving Rex one more look over his shoulder, as he spoke into his sleeve and touched his earpiece again. He slowly walked away for a few steps, seemed to listen to something being said in the earpiece, stopped and then walked back to Rex.

"Very good, Triple Sevens. They're waiting for you at the house. Please keep your headgear on until you can put on your masks." The suit guy pulled a piece of flat magnetized metal out of his jacket pocket and applied it to the license plate of his motorcycle. Please keep this on the vehicle until you leave the property and enjoy your evening." He handed the key back to Rex, nodded, climbed into the SUV and moved it out of the way so Rex and Lucy could ride past.

Rex mumbled "Triple Sevens" to himself inside the helmet and chuckled. He kept the bike moving slowly up the hill and parked next to a red Mercedes SL that also had some kind of magnetic plate attached to the license plate—in fact, all the vehicles had them.

He parked, waited for Lucy to dismount and then did the same. He pulled the paper masks out of the saddlebags, handed one to Lucy and put the other one on himself after pulling the helmet off. He had used scissors to widen the mouth holes so they could eat and drink without taking them off. He was dressed all in black like a good dungeon master or biker would be and had included a black leather vest in his ensemble.

He had found some leather wrist cuffs in his toy box, which he now gave Lucy to wear. She was also wearing tight black pants that resembled leather, a tight, scoop-necked top, and dangerously high heels. Neither of them was revealing a lot of flesh or breaking any new ground in fetish wear but Rex felt confident they could both pass through whoever or whatever was waiting for them at the check-in table. He wrapped his hand around the doorknob, looked at Lucy and said, "Ready?" She nodded as Rex twisted the knob and stepped confidently into the foyer.

The grim reaper stood in the center of the room waiting for them. The reaper was hooded, cloaked, and wearing elaborate face paint that made it impossible to know what he really looked like.

"Welcome to the Coiled Whip, Triple Sevens, and welcome to you, guest of Triple Sevens. You are required to serve the society as Dungeon Master from nine to ten o'clock this evening. Do you accept this responsibility?"

"Um, yes. I do, Mr. Reaper."

The Reaper smiled, proving that someone in the group had a sense of humor, Rex thought to himself.

"You can call me Grim, Sevens. I'm sure if you are here, you are familiar with standard dungeon protocol based on the three S's of sane, safe and consensual."

"That's technically only two S's, but yes, this is not my first trip to the rodeo."

"Outstanding. Hopefully, you have some circus experience as well. And you, young lady. As the guest of Triple Sevens, you are required to remain masked at all times and follow your host's lead at all times. Any infraction of any rule at any time means immediate expulsion. Is that understood?"

"Yes, your Reaperhood," Lucy said, as both Rex and Grim stifled a laugh.

"Very well. You may both proceed, and if you maintain your dungeon well you may be asked to join our group, Triple Sevens. I bid you good night and much luck with your duties." The Reaper bowed ever so slightly and motioned to a room to the right that had a bar in the corner.

"Cocktails?" Rex said through the mask.

"Absolutely," answered Lucy, as she walked toward the bar.

A large muscular dude wearing only a black leather harness strapped around his torso and a skull-hugging hood that covered his entire head was tending the bar. He looked Lucy and Rex in the eye and said, "How may I serve you, sir and madam?"

Rex surveyed the stock and spied a bourbon bottle he recognized. "Two bourbon and sodas, slave-boy, and make it snappy."

The bartender jumped at the command and began to mix the drinks. Lucy leaned into Rex and said, "Slave-boy?"

Rex leaned an elbow on the bar and said in a low voice, "We're trying to blend in here, remember?" Rex could see other small groups of people in costumes and masks clumped around in the other rooms that were visible. There was quiet conversation, occasional outbursts of laughter and classical piano music was coming from speakers he couldn't see. It could have been just another cocktail party in just another house except for the wardrobes and face paint.

The bartender finished the drink order and slid the sweating glasses toward Rex and Lucy. Rex instinctively reached for his wallet and looked for a tip jar. There was no jar but there was a neatly hand-lettered sign that said, "TIPS," and next to it on the bar lay a full-length rattan cane. Rex looked at the cane, and then looked at the bartender who was looking at Rex with a hopeful look in his eye.

"Seriously?" asked Rex.

"Quite serious, sir."

"Come out here and take your position," Rex said as he picked up the cane and waggled it to test the weight.

The bartender came out from behind the bar, turned his back to Rex and bent over at the waist. This revealed more male buttocks than Rex really wanted to see, but it was too late to turn back now.

"What do you consider a fair tip for your substandard level of service, slave?"

"That is not for me to say, sir. I live only to serve."

"I see," Rex said. "Well, if we were in a fancy club that would probably be twenty dollars worth of drinks and twenty percent would be four but let's round up to five. Count them off, worm."

Rex drew the cane back, gave Lucy a quick look and let the dude have it right across the middle of the cheeks. The sound of cane hitting flesh cracked through the room and things went silent for a second as the other guests reacted to the sound. The bartender said, "One," in a firm, steady voice. Rex drew the cane back for a second strike, a thin red welt was already starting to form from the first whack. Rex knew from experience that the pain from a caning didn't reach full strength until several seconds after the blow, so he stood there patiently waiting and looking over his shoulder to see who might be watching.

He could see some of the guests looking his way as he pulled back and leveled another blow, perhaps a bit harder than the first. "Two," the bartender said. He sounded like he might be breathing harder than normal, attempting to work through the pain. Rex adjusted his mask slightly and reset his feet waiting for the wave of agony to wash through the submissive before him.

He now sensed people around him and turned around to see a few of the other guests, decked out in costumes and masks watching him. Rex looked at their body shapes trying to determine if one could be the general in disguise. The guy closest to Rex was dressed in a colonial get-up, complete with breeches, buckled shoes, a silk waistcoat, vest, pirate-like shirt and a tri-cornered hat with a veil hanging from the front that obscured the guy's face with dark lace.

"Was his service flawed, my lord?" said the guy in the veil.

Rex turned to him and said, "Actually, his service was fine, but he is working for tips and this is what the scum prefers. Stand aside, my friend."

Rex pulled back and swung again, once again increasing the strength of the swing, which caused the bartender to cry out, "Ahh!" before croaking, "Three!" through his splendid misery.

Rex checked the progress of the welts and noticed the colonial guy's date was also decked out as a daughter of the revolution except for a plunging neckline that displayed some impressive cleavage. Her veil hung from a pearled headpiece that rested crown-like on her blonde-tressed head.

"Would you mind if I had a go at him?" asked the guy in the hat.

Rex felt his voice catch in his throat as he swallowed and tried not to lose his temper. Here he was at an upper echelon party in the middle of his very first scene and some dickwad was going to insert himself into the situation without being invited. This behavior, although appearing harmless and playful, was a clear violation of just about every rule in the book of kink.

Rex moved into the dude's personal space, lowered his voice and said, "Is this your first time at this kind of party, pal?"

The guy clearly stopped to think for half a second and said with an icy tone, "Not hardly, friend."

"Me neither, and where I come from, polite people don't barge into other people's scenes and ask to take over. Are you feeling me?"

The colonial guy bowed in an overly dramatic fashion and said, "Deepest apologies, my lord, please carry on."

Rex was now a bit pissed off as he drew back and struck again, the sound of cane on flesh echoing through the room.

"Four, sir," said the bartender, his voice sounding strained.

Rex held his position and silently counted some seconds wondering if the bartender had absorbed enough. He twirled the cane in his fingers and said, "I hope you've enjoyed receiving this gratuity as much as I have dispensing it."

"Indeed I have, sir, but I believe you owe me one more."

Rex arched an eyebrow and said half under his breath, "Plucky boy, aren't we?" He pulled back and cracked him again this time a bit harder than the others and tossed the cane on top of the bar. "Class dismissed," Rex said as he guided Lucy out of the room. "Come along, darling. There is much work to do." They pushed through the small crowd of people gathered to watch the proceedings.

A guy dressed an elaborate eagle costume complete with face paint and feathered wings grabbed Rex by the arm as he passed and said into his ear, "Well-played, Triple Sevens—you are doing well."

Rex nodded at the dude, who was too short to be the general. He and Lucy walked into the next room, which was set up with tables of food. There were steaming chafing dishes in the middle filled with steamed vegetables, beef wellington, and whipped potatoes. On two tables flanking the main spread of food were individual pieces of sushi and sashimi, artistically displayed on two naked women serving as human trays.

Rex had seen it done before but never with such attractive bodies or with so many different varieties of fish. Lucy gently yanked his arm and said, "What the hell is this, naked sushi night?" Rex chuckled and said, "Are you hungry?"

"I can eat something. What are you supposed to do, just take the pieces off them?"

"Yep, the more we eat, the more exposed they become. I've seen this before but it usually doesn't look this good. Come on, let's get some." There were small bowls of wasabi, two vials of soy sauce—one containing the low sodium variety, and stacks of wrapped chopsticks. Lucy picked up a set, and then perused the choices before diving down for a thick slice of pink, fatty tuna.

"Oh, my god, this is like melting in my mouth."

"Pretty classy affair, huh?" Rex said. He scanned the room, once again searching for anybody big enough to be the general but coming up empty. Lucy helped herself to a piece of salmon as Rex noticed a professionally produced sign directing them with an arrow to "At Her Feet." Rex observed the party people, scanning body types for the general and waited for Lucy to have a few more pieces of sushi. He looked at her and said, "Ready? I think you'll like the next room."

"Promises, promises," she said. Let's go."

They were greeted at the next door by a hairy-armed man wearing a nurses uniform consisting of a white dress, white nurses shoes, white hose, and a surgical mask.

"Good evening," he said while zeroing in on Lucy. "Is the young lady ready for her appointment?"

"What appointment?" Lucy said.

"Well, tonight we're offering full pedicure service with your choice of finish on the nails. We have all the popular colors—or clear, of course. And it's all offered as a complimentary service."

"Are you saying free pedicures?" asked Lucy.

Rex looked over the nurse's shoulder and saw five chairs resting on six-inch platforms lining the walls. Below each chair were footbaths, an array of nail polishes and tools that he didn't recognize, and three other men serving as nail technicians. The costumes included a stylized auto mechanic, a surgeon and one guy dressed in basic black and a black apron that made him look like a hair stylist. All of them sported the same surgical mask.

"Seriously?" Lucy said. "Free pedicures? No weird stuff?"

The nurse gave her a quick look up and down. "We are all professionals here, young lady, and it will only get weird if you want it to. But I can pretty much guarantee the best Pedi you've ever had."

"Okay, I'll play," Lucy said. "Where do I sit?"

"While you do this, I'll take a walk through the rest of the rooms," Rex said. He checked his watch.

"Okay," Lucy said. "I think I'm in safe hands here."

Rex watched as the nurse helped Lucy into a chair and then knelt to remove her boots. He walked through the kitchen, which was buzzing with catering staff who were all wearing some kind of a chef's get-up with faces obscured by white linen napkins tied around their heads—western bandit style. He caught a glimpse of another sign near the backdoor pointing toward the outdoors that read "Whipping of the Wives."

Rex swallowed, took a deep breath and pushed through the door just as the crack of a single tail whip ignited the air. A large, round tent had been set up in the backyard and the sidewalls were up, preventing anybody from seeing in. Rex walked around the perimeter as the cracks from the whip continued in a slow measured cadence. Halfway around the back, he found another sign nailed to a post stuck in the ground that silently announced, "Entrance."

Rex pulled the curtains of fabric open and stepped inside. The interior was well lit by overhead spotlights. A heavy beamed rack stood in the middle and a naked woman wearing an eye mask, arms stretched overhead, was tethered to the crossbar. Her torso was already striped with vivid red welts as a burly dude with no shirt wearing a fabric hood, jodhpurs and high black boots reared back and expertly placed the end of the whip on the back of the woman's thigh while the crack of leather rang through the night air. Her body instinctively jerked away from the pain but her legs were tied at the ankles and thighs, preventing her from moving too far in any direction.

A crowd of costumed males and females stood in a circle watching and clearly enjoying the proceedings. Some of them were smoking cigars and swilling brandy as the attractive woman in the middle of the circle absorbed the punishment while writhing and twisting. The performance unfolded like a macabre ballet out of a demon's nightmare, but Rex felt himself enjoying the spectacle.

He wondered who the woman was. Was the dude with the whip her husband, or had the husband hired the sadist so he could watch and enjoy the show? The blows continued to rain down as Rex began silently counting them in his head while slowly walking around the circle checking out the spectators, trying to gauge whether one of them could be the guy that everybody was so interested in.

Some were dressed as kinked-up cowboys. There were biker-types, pirates, and primitives wearing animal skins and brown leather loincloths. Everybody wore some kind of a mask including a guy in a priest's outfit, complete with a collar, cloak and a Hamburg style black hat. Nobody looked like the general, at least not that he could recognize. Rex made his way slowly around the circle checking out naked behinds poking through chaps and well-toned arms snaking out of leather vests. This was certainly the most attractive collection of kinksters that Rex had ever seen gathered in one location. But he still wasn't seeing who he was looking for.

He walked back inside and noticed a sign pointing toward what must be the basement door, which read "Dungeon." "Well, of course," he said to himself, "where else would it be?" He decided to check out the rest of the rooms first and found his way to the stairs to the second level. He looked through toward the front room and could tell from the sounds and the people gathered that the bartender was grunting through another round of being appropriately tipped.

Rex walked up the steps slowly toward the master suite and saw a sign that said "Service by Sissy Boys." He decided to peek in and was met at the door by a tall man in a ballerina costume complete with a swan-like headpiece, make-up, and tutu. "Good evening, sir—is there anything we can do for you?"

Rex looked past the guy's shoulder to see three guys each sitting on one side of the bed. One was wearing some kind of military uniform while what appeared to be a woman knelt between his legs, head bobbing in his crotch. Another guy had his back to him but he could tell that he was being serviced in a similar way.

The third guy was decked out in a slightly tacky suit with matching hat in the style of a 1920's gangster. A figure wearing a full-length, slinky cocktail dress was on their knees in front of him and there was a good deal of coital sounding noise coming from the bathroom as flesh slapped against flesh.

"Ummm, I don't think so, sweety. I'm kind of looking for some friends of mine. Three guys, one of them pretty big, maybe they came in together? Not sure how they're dressed, maybe as military dudes like the guy on the bed. Does that ring any bells with you?"

The guy licked his lips a bit too obviously and said, "Can't say as it does, sugar. Maybe you need to take a closer look?"

"Mmm, no thanks. I'm good. I'll keep looking. Looks like you boys are doing some fine work here, though."

"Well, we aim to please. Come on back if you change your mind, and I'll prove it to you."

"I'm sure you would," Rex said as he turned away and walked past some other bedrooms, some of which had hotel-style "Do Not Disturb" signs hanging on the doorknobs. One door stood ajar as a group stood around a king-sized bed watching two nude women and a shirtless man groping, thrusting, and moaning. From his vantage point, he couldn't tell who was doing what to whom.

Rex turned away and headed back downstairs. He peeked his head into the foot fetish room and saw that Lucy was now choosing colors and seemed to be very comfortable. He made his way to the basement door and slowly stepped down the darkened steps. There was another bar set up in the far corner and there were a few masters and slaves hanging out. Both walls of the main room were lined with an impressive variety of racks, restraints, and benches. A Saint Andrews cross was occupied by a damsel in distress dressed as a harem girl with her top pulled down, as a dude in a stylized cop uniform squeezed and sucked at her breasts.

Rex checked his watch, aware that his shift was about to start, and looked for the dungeon master currently on duty. A skinny, bearded guy in a black t-shirt with multiple and intricate ear piercings was standing off to the side watching the proceedings. He was wearing a lone-ranger style mask. Rex stepped up to him and said, "Excuse me, masked man. Are you the dungeon master?"

"I am," he said, looking Rex up and down. "Are you a twisted mime or my relief or both?"

"Tonight, I am both. Is there anything special I need to be aware of?"

"No, it's a pretty well-behaved and sophisticated crowd. The dungeon usually runs itself. I do try to keep a watchful eye on the edge room. That's where the real perverts hang out."

The dude jerked his head toward a hallway that Rex hadn't noticed. "Oh really? What's the big attraction in there?"

"You know, the usual stuff. Some needlework, knife guys, we tried doing fire for awhile the but the ceilings aren't really tall enough and then we usually get some chokers."

"Chokers?"

"You know, erotic asphyxiation? They have ropes and nooses set up and they go in there and choke each other out. Way too freaky for my tastes but a lot of people dig it."

"Yeah, not my thing either. Is that area considered part of the dungeon? I mean am I supposed to be watching that shit too?"

"Just poke your head in occasionally. Maybe they won't show up tonight and you won't have to worry about it."

"Who's they?"

"The chokers, man, the chokers. They're really the only ones that make me nervous. Are you ready to take over now? Because I could really use a drink."

Rex checked his watch and figured Lucy was going to be occupied for a while so he gave the guy a clap on the shoulder and said, "Sure, I got this."

The guy slipped away as Rex took his position, which gave him a view of the whole room. Nobody seemed to be in any obvious distress, so he shifted his feet and settled in for the hour. Just as his mind started to wander, movement from the steps caught his eye. He turned to see a woman with a burlap hood over her head and her hands tied behind her back being led by the upper arm toward the edge room. Rex assumed it was a kidnapping scene, some of which could be pretty elaborate. The guy guiding the girl was big, and he moved through the space slowly and deliberately like he was afraid of breaking something, but at the same time, Rex could sense tension as they walked past.

Rex gauged the guy's height and decided it could be the general. The guy was wearing a white jumpsuit with an oversized zipper down the front, pockets on the sleeves and legs, and a rubber mask of Richard Nixon.

The guy didn't give Rex a second look as he guided the petite, trim girl, who was wearing a short white skirt and high heels, past him and maneuvered her into the room. Rex took a slow stroll around the dungeon, pretending to be supervising the proceedings as got closer to the edge room door—just as it closed in front of his face. He listened for a second for the sound of a lock being thrown and was relieved when it didn't happen. But the closed door still intrigued and concerned him.

He decided to wait for a few minutes to let them get started into whatever it was they were going to do. He pulled out his phone and texted Lucy.

"I'm in the dungeon doing my duty. Everything okay up there?"

A few minutes later she responded with, "Yes, I'm fine; toes look great—they're all taking pictures and fighting over who gets to massage them."

"She may learn to like this stuff," Rex said under his breath.

He took another turn around the room, making sure nobody was tied too tightly. He got back to the door to the edge room, put his hand on the knob and slowly turned it. He pushed the door open and was flooded with revulsion, fear, and anger by the site of the girl hanging from a noose around her neck. The other end of the rope went through an eyebolt that was screwed into a wooden rack stretching across the space.

The woman was up on her toes and the guy in the jumpsuit was holding onto the rope, pulling on it, trying to make it tighter. He was totally focused on what he was doing and hadn't heard Rex come in. Rex stepped out of the doorway and slid behind a pillar, partially hiding from view. The girl was clearly struggling to breathe as the jumpsuit guy started to slowly pull down the zipper on his suit. He had the upper body of an athlete, big-chested and thick-necked.

Rex kept his eye on the girl, whose hands were tied with what looked like a necktie. As the seconds ticked by, her motions to find slack in the rope and draw a breath became more pronounced. Rex felt beads of perspiration form on his forehead. He scanned the rest of the room for other participants, but they were alone. There was a workbench up against the far wall and Rex could see some random restraint devices and sex toys scattered around the top of it.

Part of his brain told him a woman was being strangled in front of his eyes, while another part of him said this was just a scene, an act of play between two consenting adults. It wasn't his job to interfere with something he didn't fully understand. He moved his mask enough to allow him to brush his forehead with the back of his hand and zeroed in on the girl's feet. Her shoes were now barely scraping the floor as she twisted and thrashed about.

The guy in the jumpsuit was holding onto the line with one hand and reaching inside his suit with the other. Rex was pretty sure what was going to happen next. It was going to be a hand on the rope and a hand on himself. He started to leave the room as a feeling of nausea washed over him. He took one more look over his shoulder and noticed the girl had stopped moving.

Instinct took over. "Hey!" Rex yelled. He rushed toward the guy in the Nixon mask. In two steps he noticed there was a single-blade, safety rope cutting tool on the workbench. He pushed the guy and tried to get a grip on the rope. "Let her down, man! She's not breathing."

The guy shoved Rex off like a bug, pointed at him and said, "Stay out of my scene, asshole. This isn't any of your business."

Rex glanced at the girl, who still wasn't moving, and decided the guy was too big to take down with a single blow. He pushed by him, grabbed the rope cutter, went back to the rope and with one motion, felt the razor sharp blade cut it in two. Rex grabbed for the loose end of the rope but hadn't anticipated the weight of the girl or the strength needed to hold her. He felt the rope burn its way into his palm as he tried to break her fall – only partially succeeding. The girl slumped to the floor. Rex knelt beside her, tore off the burlap mask, and loosened the rope around her neck.

"Sheena! Holy shit!"

Rex rested her head on the floor, noticed she was turning blue and pumped her chest a few times just as a blinding, white flash appeared in his skull.

He became aware that he was on his back on the floor staring up at Richard Nixon, who was holding a heavy rubber baton smeared with blood.

"What the fuck is the matter with you, sport? You've never seen edge before? There's nothing wrong with her. I'll have you banned. You need to mind your own business."

Rex touched the side of his head and felt blood. He rolled onto his side and held up a hand to ward off any more blows. "Sorry, dude." In his wounded state, he wondered if he had gone over the line. Was she really okay? He pulled his mask over his head to see better and turned to look at Sheena, who was now coughing while struggling to sit up.

"Are you okay?" Rex said.

"This asshole's trying to kill me," Sheena said.

"Bullshit, you little bitch! You consented!" shouted the guy through the mask.

"Not to be fucking strangled!" yelled Sheena. She craned her neck trying to get more slack in the rope.

Rex struggled to his knees while shaking his head, trying to come to his senses. Once he made up his mind about who was right, he got to his feet and took a running start toward the guy in the jumpsuit. He lowered his shoulder and drove himself into the guy's gut. Rex heard the wind rush out of him. He clambered and clawed his way onto the top of him, reached for the guy's mask and pulled it over his head.

"Well, well, well, if it isn't General Hap Patterson," Rex said.

The guy immediately freed his arm, grabbed Rex by the throat, and started squeezing. "Always in the wrong place at the wrong time, aren't you, sport?" Rex tried to pull the general's hand away, but he was way too strong, and once again things started to get fuzzy inside his skull. He raised a fist and brought it down on the bridge of the general's nose, which caused him to cry out, but the grip only tightened.

Rex sensed movement behind him and was able to see out of the corner of his eye that the grim reaper had entered the room. He moved closer and deftly stepped onto the general's throat with a lizard-skinned, pointy-toed cowboy boot. "Cease and desist, sir, or I shall crush your windpipe like a dry twig."

Rex looked down and saw genuine concern on the general's face. "He's a newbie." His voice was coming out in dry croaks. "He fucked up my scene. You know me. Throw this asshole out!" The grip on Rex's throat tightened again.

Rex watched the reaper bear down a bit harder, "I'm not kidding, number 23. Release him and I assure you we'll get to the bottom of this."

The vise on his throat loosened and Rex stood up, hacking. He now realized several other costumed participants had entered the edge room. The reaper removed his boot from the general and knelt in front of Sheena.

"Are you hurt?" he asked.

"No. But I did think he was going to strangle me," she said.

"Are your hands bound?"

Sheena half-turned to show her raw red wrists tied together with a navy blue necktie.

Rex scanned the masked faces in the room, trying to get a handle on what was going to happen next, just as Lucy pushed her way through the crowd. Rex stood up. In a lowered voice he said to her, "Come on, we need to get out of here." He put his hand on her shoulder and began to ease her toward the door. He turned back and now noticed that the guy in the priest costume had come forward and was looking down at the general as he rubbed his neck and stood up.

"You are unmasked, sir. A clear violation."

The general pointed at Rex and yelled, "Yeah, because that asshole attacked me in the middle of a scene." Rex stopped, quickly pulled his mask back down, and turned to face his accuser. "I thought he was going to kill her. She had stopped breathing."

The priest looked at Rex and with a hand gesture that looked somehow familiar, and waved him off. The priest turned toward the reaper as the general picked himself off the floor and tried to insert himself into the conversation. Rex didn't wait for a second invitation and quickly guided Lucy up the stairs toward the front door.

"What the hell was happening down there?" she said.

"It was the general. He almost fucking killed Sheena."

"Sheena, the girl you were at the bar with? I thought she looked familiar."

"Yeah, I don't know what she was doing here. I didn't think she was coming."

"Did you ask her to come to this with you before me?"

"No, of course not."

Rex readjusted his mask as they made their way back through the house, the other partygoers turning into a blur of kinkery as they walked by.

"So now what? Are we done here?" asked Lucy.

"Yep," Rex said. "I'm not sure how this is going to shake itself out but I believe our jobs are finished."

After they got outside Rex pulled out his cellphone and called Detective Span.

"Hello, Detective. I'm just leaving the party I told you about. Didn't see the French guy, but I did see U.S. Army General Hap Patterson almost choke a chick to death with a noose. Her hands were tied behind her back with a blue necktie. I certainly hope this helps, makes your day and causes you to leave me the fuck alone. I'm currently leaving the site, as far as I know, the general is still in there if you'd like to talk to him."

Rex put the phone back in his pocket and walked to the bike in a daze. He wiped some blood off his forehead and examined the wound using the mirror on the bike but it looked minor. His mind drifted as he navigated back toward the city and he was grateful for the sound of the wind surrounding them in a white noise of silence. He walked Lucy back to her apartment door. She unlocked it and said, "Well, Rex, thanks for another one of the craziest nights I've ever had. At least I got myself an excellent pedicure. Those guys"

Rex didn't let her finish and instead pushed his lips to hers, feeling the soft flesh on his. She tensed at his sudden movement, but then he felt her body relax slightly as he pulled back and looked into her eyes.

"I've been wanting to do that for a long time," he said. She started to say something but he held up a finger. "Let me finish. I'm really sorry I dragged you into all this freaky stuff, because I'm really crazy about you, Lucy. I always have been. I know we're friends and neighbors and drinking buddies, but I think you're really awesome and I really would like to take you on a real date, with no intrigue or drama—if you'll go with me."

She didn't say anything for seconds that felt like hours and then said, "You certainly know how to keep a girl guessing. Hold that thought and give me a call, next week, on the phone after all the dust settles, okay? But in the meantime, here's something to think about."

She tilted her head and kissed him back, their lips parting and melting into passion as Rex put his arms around her, pulling her close. He felt a deep excitement and yearning, but he willed himself to hold back and released her. "I think I'm finished with this whole kink scene, too. I don't need all that weird stuff to have a good time if I'm with the right girl."

She smiled at him and cocked her head. "Are you sure about that, Rex? If you learned how to do pedicures like those boys do, I might hold onto you forever and ever." She unlocked the door and blew him a kiss as he stood there and watched it close. He rode the elevator down to his floor, peeled off his clothes, and slept more soundly than he had in weeks.

CHAPTER 18

Rex spent the rest of the weekend doing as little as possible. He texted Sheena to make sure she was okay, which she was and then sent a message to Wellborn requesting a debriefing. He didn't hear a word from the cops, which he took as good news. He felt good about his little speech to Lucy and decided to wait and let his words sink in before following up with her. If she rejected him, he anticipated a certain amount of heartache, but at least he had made his feelings known. Hopefully whatever happened or didn't happen between them wouldn't impact his deep friendship and attraction for her.

Wellborn responded and proposed a lunch on Monday. Rex intended to use it to get to the bottom of everything he'd seen and experienced. Sunday evening melted into a gray Monday morning. He had a lot of questions and was counting on Wellborn having the answers. A general staff meeting at work that ended a few minutes before lunchtime took up most of his morning. He put his PC to sleep and headed to the regular spot, where he found Wellborn at his regular table, back to the wall and facing the front door.

"Ahh…Mr. Armstrong. Greetings and felicitations. Tell us the news," Wellborn said as Rex took his regular seat.

"Actually I was hoping you could do that," Rex said, "because I'm still not exactly sure what all that meant."

"Well, first things first." Wellborn reached into his inside jacket pocket and pulled out a plastic zip lock bag with a stainless steel ring in it that looked very familiar.

"Is that my…?"

"It is your property recovered from the Metro Police Department, which now has no further use for it."

Rex took the bag and stuffed it into his pocket. "Meaning…?"

"Their current theory, one that I agree with, is that this bit of evidence fell from or was plucked from your pocket after you were knocked unconscious in the parking lot of the fetish club. It was then planted on your unfortunate friend Amy, to make it look like you had something to do with her death."

"I see," Rex said. "And the person who did the planting was…"

"Probably, sorry to say, U.S. General Hap Patterson, who was linked to the navy blue neckties used to bind both Amy's and the very lucky Sheena's wrists."

"I see, and François was what, his accomplice?"

"Actually, Rex, François works for us. That's why the Metropolitan Police couldn't find him even when they had his cellphone."

"Works for us? François does?"

Wellborn nodded and ordered the grilled cheese and tomato soup combo. Rex went with a cheesesteak sandwich with everything.

"But François was the guy who gave me the key," Rex said. "The key that got me into the Coiled Whip event."

Wellborn gracefully dropped his napkin on his lap. "And?"

"And so if he works for 'us,' whoever us is, how did he get the key?"

"Let's just say we have people working for us from all walks of life and assuming all manner of appearances."

"As in, draped in the vestments of a priest?" Rex asked.

Wellborn did one of his wiggling finger gestures. "Who knows? Maybe we have a few holy men on the payroll. Even I don't know everybody."

Rex was surprised how everything Wellborn said seemed to be totally implausible and yet was making perfect sense. "So what about the French and the drone technology and all that?"

"All fabrication, Rex. The French have their own drone technology. They routinely invite top U.S. military members to their functions, hoping that in case said officers retire and go to work for defense contractors, knowing them will help them sell more arms overseas. It's just the way the arms business works."

"So you lied to me in order to get me to do these things."

Wellborn picked up the butter knife and twisted it around in his fingertips. "Now, Rex. You did these things on your own volition to make money to pay off your debt to the IRS. At least, that's what you told me. I gave you a cover story that you could use in case you got caught, which you did, and then proceeded to, as they say, 'spill your guts' to anybody who would listen to you. The cover story was to protect you, me, and them."

"You could have just told me the truth. I'm a big boy."

"Yes you are, but since we hadn't really worked together before, we had to take a few precautions along the way."

"Another test? Like the whole Metro thing?"

"Exactly and, oh, by the way, nobody is stealing Metro funds, either. That was another cover story we used."

Rex stared off into space, letting it all sink in for a second, before saying, "Quite a little web of deceit and trickery you have going on here, Mr. Wellborn."

"Just doing my job, Mr. Armstrong."

"And I guess that's the one question that remains unanswered, isn't it? What is your job and who exactly are you working for?"

Wellborn spread some butter onto a carved-up roll and said, "Well, that's easy. I work for the American people."

"By spying on and deceiving innocent people?"

Wellborn put the knife on the table. "Technically they are not all innocent. The general is probably going to be charged with a crime, probably murder, as well he should. But I'm glad you're bringing this up with all the hoo-hah going on about who we're spying on and why vis-à-vis privacy laws and what-have-you. What people seem to be forgetting is that spies spy on people, guilty and innocent, because that is the spy's job. We're in the intelligence business. We gather data, sometimes in ways that are unsavory—but this is an unsavory world. It would be wonderful to have an existence where everybody got along and played by the rules and everybody respected everybody's civil rights, but unfortunately, that is not reality. The reality is there are a lot of bad guys out there bent on doing bad things to nice people like you and me, and sometimes, the only way to find them is by spying on them."

"That's a great justification for doing just about anything, legal or illegal, isn't it?"

"I sleep well most nights and I can only hope that you do as well, Mr. Armstrong. On behalf of your country, I thank you for your assistance in this matter, and here is the agreed-on fee for your last and final mission. I'd say there's also a good chance that you won't be hearing from the IRS again."

Wellborn held out an envelope as Rex slowly reached across the table. He could tell from the feel that it was made from the usual high-quality paper stock. He slipped it into jacket pocket.

"My final mission?"

"I'd say the case is closed at this point, yes."

"And you won't be needing help on other cases?"

"Not that I anticipate. Thank you for your service."

Rex looked down at the table, studying the pattern of the linen tablecloth. He breathed out and felt a mixture of relief and disappointment.

"I have to admit, I kind of liked it."

"That doesn't surprise me, Rex. It's part of your profile."

"Mmm-hmm..."

Wellborn was eyeing the food that arrived and Rex assumed that the discussion of his part-time job was over. They finished the meal bantering about sports and local politics. Rex gave him a solid handshake and headed back to his regular life. He got back to his office and texted Lucy.

"Have any plans for Saturday night?"

A few minutes later she responded.

"Yes. Lots of kinky sex with you."

Rex laughed to himself, laid the phone on the desk, and began thinking about where he was going to take Lucy on their first real date.

About the Author

Scott Sowers grew up in northeastern Ohio and began pitching stories to magazines while still in high school. He's worked as a boat salesman, bartender, television producer, journalist, and a reporter. When not writing fiction he writes about real estate, energy, and the automotive world. His work appears in The Washington Post, The Atlantic and The New York Times.